ME NOT

Boss
ME NOT

AJ RANNEY

Rudy House Publishing

Boss Me Not

A Man of the Month Novella

Copyright @ 2025 A.J. Ranney

Developmental & Line Edit by Michelle Fewer

Copy, Proofreading by Beth Lawton at VB Edits

Cover by Matilda Martel

ISBN: 978-1-965124-07-9 (ebook)

ISBN: 978-1-965124-11-6 (paperback)

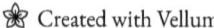 Created with Vellum

To Kara, Annie, and all of the Man of the Month authors!

Listen on Spotify!

God Gave Me A Girl - Russell Dickerson
Yours - Russell Dickerson
Gorgeous - Brett Eldredge
You For A Reason - Warren Zeiders
Work On Me - Restless Road
Are You Even Real - Teddy Swims, GIVEON
Lose Control - Teddy Swims
I Choose You - Forest Blakk
All Of The Girls You Loved Before - Taylor Swift
King Of My Heart - Taylor Swift
Gonna Love You - Parmalee
Dancing In The Rain - Chase Matthew

Prologue

ANGIE

I STARED at my phone as the hotel's number flashed across the screen. Why was Blanche calling? I hoped she hadn't decided that I was underqualified for the job after all. Even if she was calling to disappoint me, I should probably answer.

"Hey, sorry." I glanced between my two best friends. "Gotta take this. It's the hotel."

They both nodded, and I headed toward Mina's bedroom, swiping the answer button and bringing the phone to my ear.

"Hello?" I stepped through the door, making sure it clicked shut quietly behind me. I didn't want an audience if she was calling to tell me she'd changed her mind and I wasn't getting the job after all.

A deep huff that sounded very male and nothing like the older woman I'd met a couple of weeks ago came through the phone.

"Angie Mitchell?" the voice finally said.

"Yes."

"It's Wyatt Reed."

Wyatt? Oh. Blanche's grandson? Why in the world was he calling me?

"My grandmother has passed away, and I—"

"What?" My voice rose two octaves. I couldn't have heard that right. I'd just seen her. She was the spunkiest seventy-something-year-old I'd ever met. "What happened?"

He sighed. "She died." His voice held quite a bit of disdain, almost laced with exasperation. "Are you still interested in the job here?"

Wow. Okay. Guess I wasn't getting any more information on the poor woman.

I took a deep breath before replying. "I am still interested. But—"

"Fine. Then I need you here by Thursday morning."

"Thursday?"

"Jesus," he muttered.

My voice might have gone a bit out of control again, but it was Monday. How did he expect me to get there in three days? "I'm on vacation. In South Carolina. I don't—"

"If you can't be here by Thursday, I'll find someone who can. It won't be hard to find someone competent who wants this job."

I gritted my teeth as I processed what he wasn't saying. He didn't think I was a good fit for the position. Which meant he knew I had very little experience in hospitality management.

But I wanted this job. More than anything. And I had no intention of letting him rip it away from me.

"I'll be there."

A sound almost like a growl came through the line. "Fine. See you then."

The call went silent, and I pulled the phone away from my ear. He hung up. The asshole ended the call. And he never told me what happened to Blanche.

Now I had to go out and tell the girls I had to cut our vacation short. I had less than three days to book a flight to Massachusetts, pack enough stuff to get me through the first week or two, and figure out where I would be staying. I wasn't supposed to move there and start for another two weeks. Hopefully they could have my apartment ready early.

I'd make it work. Because once I put my mind to a goal, there was nothing stopping me. And I would prove to Wyatt that I was more than competent.

Chapter One

ANGIE

I EYED the hotel as we pulled to a stop in front of it. At least Wyatt had sent a car to pick me up from the airport. Maybe this wouldn't be too bad. Even if demanding someone start a job almost two weeks earlier than originally discussed had asshole written all over it.

The car door opened, and I swung my feet out, tugging my black skirt back down over my thighs and taking the driver's offered hand.

"Thank you." I swallowed down the nerves that threatened to bubble up into my throat.

When Blanche hired me, I hadn't been nervous—about

accepting the hotel manager position or moving to Starlight Bay. She'd been super down-to-earth and laid back, not once bringing up the fact that I was likely underqualified for the job. I was only twenty-four, a year post college, and had only three months of restaurant management experience under my belt.

But instead, she'd repeated over and over how perfect I was for the position.

Now, though, the fact that I had zero experience running a hotel and would be stuck working for her grandson left me a ball of nerves. I had no place to live for two weeks because my rental couldn't be ready early, and I still had to go home and pack up the rest of my stuff. Change didn't bother me if it was planned and within my control. But chaos wasn't my jam, and this had hot mess written all over it. It had me questioning why I thought moving somewhere new would be fun.

"Right this way, miss," the driver said before turning and wheeling my two bags toward the front entrance.

My heels clicked on the cement as we approached the doors. I glanced up at the four-story mostly brick building. Like the first time I was here, it took my breath away. The Victorian-style structure had a full wraparound veranda that led to a huge gazebo on one side. It was gorgeous. The cupolas added to the beauty.

We stepped through the large red doors and were greeted by a young guy in a navy blue suit whose name tag read *Steven*.

"Can you show her to Wyatt's office?" The driver passed my luggage off. "And have her luggage sent up to his room?"

His room. What did he mean? "You mean my room?"

The tall man with salt-and-pepper hair shook his head. "No. The hotel is completely booked because of a large wedding, so Wyatt said you'll be staying in his suite with him."

Steven handed off my bags to a young woman.

"I—" The last thing I wanted to do was share any space with

that asshole. But my new apartment wasn't ready, and if there were no rooms vacant in the hotel, did I have another choice? Maybe the inn we'd passed on our way through town had a vacancy. Before I could object, Steven turned, heading toward the front desk.

"Follow me."

My lips lifted into a smile as we passed a table with a beautiful flower arrangement centered on it. The lobby was bright and colorful, decorated with various art pieces, flowers, and throw pillows on most of the chairs and sofas. I focused on Steven and continued to follow him down the hallway that led back to the staff area.

I swallowed nervously again as he knocked on a slightly open door. The last time I'd stepped into this office, I had been excited about the possibilities.

"Come in," a deep voice called in reply.

Steven pushed the door open, waving me in front of him. I took a deep breath and stepped inside.

"Angie Mitchell for you, sir."

"Thank you, Steven." Wyatt stood and slid his hands into the pockets of his black trousers. "You can close the door behind you."

The door clicked shut, and I shifted on my heels, suddenly feeling intimidated. Wyatt was almost a foot taller than my five-foot-three frame and way better-looking than Google had led me to believe. And yes, I'd googled him. Well, not specifically him, but when Blanche invited me to come for an interview, I wanted to be prepared. Not my fault her grandson happened to pop up as well.

I'd found out from my search that his parents had both come from wealthy families, which made him wealthy as well. But it had been Blanche who'd told me she'd raised him after both his mom and dad died in a plane crash when he was five. Out of my peripheral, I eyed the same large portrait that had prompted that conversation. It was of Blanche, her husband, and a ten-year-old Wyatt.

I took in the man standing in front of me again before he cleared his throat, and my gaze snapped to his face. Heat flooded my cheeks. Dammit, I'd been caught staring at the bare skin where the top two buttons of his dress shirt were undone.

Great job, Angie. Checking out the boss on your first day. I held back a groan as a smirk lifted his lips. Not just any smirk, but one that dripped with sex appeal. And one that said he knew it too.

Chapter Two

WYATT

"WASN'T SURE YOU WERE COMING." Frankly, I still couldn't fathom why my grandmother had hired her. Other than a minor in business, she had no qualifications. She had little experience in management and zero experience working in a hotel. But I was stuck. Because in good old Nana B fashion, she'd made sure I couldn't get rid of this chick. Ninety days was what the stupid stipulation in the will said. I wasn't allowed to fire her before then.

"I told you I was." She crossed her arms, and her full breasts lifted into the scoop of her blue shirt.

I tore my gaze away and back to her face. It didn't matter that she had the type of curves any man would fantasize about. She'd still be a thorn in my side for the next three months.

Feigning complete indifference, I shrugged. "You weren't happy when I said I needed you here."

Her caramel-colored eyes rolled. "I don't think anyone would be happy if their boss demanded they end their vacation and start two weeks earlier than originally agreed upon." She barely took a breath. "And what's with the room situation? I am not staying with you. I want my own space. If there's no space here, I'll go check at the inn down the road."

"You can check, but I doubt they have anything either. There are three weddings here this weekend. And it's not necessary. The owner's suite has two bedrooms and two bathrooms."

She sighed and glanced away, shifting on her feet again.

"I promise it's plenty big enough. Probably won't even see each other." Why the fuck was I even trying so hard? If she didn't want to stay in the suite, she could go find other accommodations. "But feel free to check at the inn if you want."

"I will."

"Okay. You're on Bridezilla duty until Sunday."

"What?" Her brows pulled together, and she cocked her head, staring at me like I needed to explain.

I swear to God, if I had to hold her hand, I was going to lose it.

"The bride? The wedding this weekend? The whole reason I needed you here?"

She narrowed her eyes. "Well, I wouldn't know that, now, would I? Because you gave me zero details. About anything." She slammed her hands onto her hips. "In fact, I had to use Google to find out what happened to Blanche."

I wasn't doing this with her. The last thing I wanted to do was recount the passing of my grandmother and the secret she'd kept.

She let out a huff, obviously catching on that I wasn't saying anything more about personal issues that weren't her business.

"Why do you need me to deal with the bride?"

"She's a lot. Not my strong suit. I have zero patience for demanding, high-maintenance women." I glared at her, already pegging her as high-maintenance too. "You two will probably get along well."

She opened her mouth but snapped it shut quickly. Interesting. She wasn't denying it.

"She's already asked the staff for one million and one things, and it hasn't even been a full day," I added.

"Blanche said the big weddings bring in lots of guests and revenue, so it's probably best we keep the bride happy."

"Yeah, yeah. But within reason." I reached up and grabbed at the back of my neck. "We are *not* painting our white chairs eggshell."

Angie chuckled, and I raised an eyebrow. She thought that was funny? At least she hadn't asked why.

I couldn't even tell the difference when the bride had shown me the swatch for eggshell. Looked white to me. Her poor husband. Exactly why I was never getting married.

"She sounds fun. I look forward to dealing with her."

I couldn't tell whether she was being sarcastic or serious. She tugged at the hem of her shirt, pulling it down and smoothing her hands down her sides, causing my gaze to zero in on her breasts playing peek-a-boo at the neckline.

I stepped around my desk and gestured toward the door. "I have an appointment with the couple and the bride's parents to go over any last-minute details. I can introduce you and let them know you'll be their contact person for the weekend."

She nodded and turned toward the door. Without permission, my gaze traveled down to the round globes of her ass that were accented perfectly in the black skirt she wore. I fought a groan as she walked out the door in front of me.

Jesus. I needed to get a grip. The last thing I should be doing was checking out my newest employee.

But almost an hour later, it wasn't only her gorgeous curves that had my attention. The way she handled herself with Bridezilla had been impressive. The bride's constant ridiculous demands made my eye twitch, but Angie took each one in stride.

"You were great with her. You have more patience than I do. I was ready to walk out of there after fifteen minutes."

She shot me a smirk as we walked back toward the lobby. "Thank you. She's a bit much, I'll give you that, but in the end, I think she just wants her special day to be perfect."

"If you say so." I didn't get it. I wasn't sure I ever would. It was basically a fancy party and not one I ever planned on having. "Let me show you the suite and you can decide if you want to check the inn or not."

"Okay."

We stepped onto the elevator a moment later, and I pushed the button for the top floor. She fidgeted with the hem of her shirt again before running her hands down the sides of her skirt, pushing it back down to her knees. Personally, I liked it better when it was bunched up and showing off a few inches of her thighs.

Fuck. I had to stop this. I could not think of Angie—no, Ms. Mitchell—in any other manner than I did the rest of my staff.

Once the doors opened and we stepped into the hallway, I pointed to the right. "There are two suites that way." Then I gestured to the left. "And mine is this way."

"The bridal party has both of the other suites, right?"

"Yup." I headed left, and she fell in step behind me. Sliding my key through the card reader, I held the door open for her.

As she brushed past me, a sweet floral scent hit my nose, and I couldn't stop from breathing her in.

"Oh wow." She looked from one wall to the other and then glanced over her shoulder at me, still frozen in the same spot. "These paintings are gorgeous. You're into art like Blanche was?"

"It was one of her passions. Something we eventually shared. As an adult, I bought her pieces, but I don't know if I have the eye for it like she did."

"Do you know what Rainbow Row is?"

I shook my head. Although it sounded familiar, I couldn't place it. Finally, I made my feet move and came to stand next to her.

"It's a row of historic houses down in Charleston that are each painted various bright, beautiful pastel colors." Her lips turned up slightly and a dimple appeared on her right cheek. "The painting downstairs in the lobby reminded me of it."

"The one with the colorful doors?"

She nodded. "It's mesmerizing—the way the background is so muted and the doors leap off the canvas."

"If I remember correctly, the painting's based on New Orleans."

"Really?" Her head tilted and the ends of her platinum blond hair brushed along her collarbone. Her red painted lips were striking against her pale skin and hair. "I've never been."

I shifted uncomfortably, willing myself to stop noticing things like how she smelled, the dimple when she smiled, her curves, or her lips. I refused to be attracted to her. My dick needed to get the memo too. Merely the idea of her had me fuming a few days ago. That was what I had to remember. I was stuck with her for three months. Whether she did a good job or not.

"The view is gorgeous."

I looked up to where she had moved toward the balcony

doors overlooking the ocean. I brought my fist to my lips as my gaze locked on her luscious ass. I was totally fucked. Because all I could think was *damn right, the view is gorgeous.*

And I didn't mean the ocean.

Chapter Three

ANGIE

I HAD TO ADMIT, Wyatt was right. His suite was huge. Probably bigger than my apartment back in Half Moon Lake and the one I would be renting here combined. I could literally sit out on the balcony all night. Between the gorgeous view of the stars in the sky and the sound of the waves crashing against the sand, it was my new favorite space. It definitely made it easier to say yes to his offer. Not that I really had a choice. The inn had nothing open until Sunday, and at that point, it would be ridiculous to go stay there for a night.

Deep in my thoughts, I almost jumped off the chair when

the door opened behind me. *Get a grip, Angie. It is his place, after all.*

"Sorry, didn't mean to scare you."

Heat crept up into my cheeks. "You didn't."

He raised an eyebrow, like he wanted to call bullshit. "Have you eaten?"

I shook my head. "Not since lunch."

After he'd shown me the suite earlier, we went downstairs to one of the conference rooms for a meeting with the restaurant, housekeeping, and security managers. He'd had the restaurant bring in a delicious lunch spread.

"I grabbed pizza from Starlight Pi, if you want some."

I was sure the food here would have me gaining weight at a rapid rate. Why did I have to love eating so much? Couldn't I be like those people who forget to eat? No, food was constantly on my mind.

"Thanks." I stood and followed him back inside to the kitchen island, where three pizza boxes sat. "Are you expecting company?"

"No. Why?"

"That's just tons of pizza for one person." Even if he assumed I hadn't eaten yet, three large pizzas were a lot for even two people.

"Oh." He shrugged. "I always order extra and leave some down in the staff lounge."

Maybe I'd read him wrong. I was still pissed that he'd demanded I come up here two weeks earlier than planned, but his actions weren't those of a self-centered jerk. Maybe he truly felt like he needed the help and couldn't handle it another week.

"Whatever we don't eat, I'll take downstairs. If you hadn't eaten yet, I wanted you to have choices."

"I like any type of pizza." Did I look like someone who would be picky about food? Not that I planned on asking him that. But seriously, my thick thighs and generous ass should have been a clear giveaway.

He handed me a plate and listed the toppings of all three pizzas.

"So many good choices." I stepped up to the island, eyeing the options before finally going with a slice of meat lovers and a slice of ham with pineapple.

"Do you want a glass of wine?" Wyatt asked. "I have Merlot and Riesling."

"Sure. Riesling is good."

He set two glasses on the granite island and turned, pulling a bottle from the small wine cooler that sat on the counter.

"Would you like to eat on the balcony?" he asked as he poured the golden-colored liquid into glasses.

"Oh, um, sure." I flinched at how awkward that sounded. Why did his presence evoke some tongue-tied version of me? "I mean, don't feel like you have to eat with me. You don't have to entertain me or anything. I don't want to be in your way or—"

He crowded my space, and suddenly, I couldn't speak. His woodsy cologne overtook my senses, and his piercing green eyes stayed locked on me. I swallowed as he leaned closer and rested his hand on the island next to me. He was so close I could make out a small, faded scar on the outer part of his right eyebrow.

"You're my guest and you're not in my way. I don't do anything unless I want to, and tonight I would love to sit and get to know you."

I shifted and my arm brushed his thumb, sending a myriad of sensations shooting through my body and straight to my core. My traitorous body must have missed the memo that this guy was now my boss. Completely off-limits.

He studied me before a smirk lifted his lips. "I feel like we got off on the wrong foot, and I'd like to make up for that."

I forced a chuckle through my lips. "You mean by demanding I drop everything and start early?"

He raised an eyebrow. "No. That part I'm not apologizing for. I needed you here early. No way was I gonna be able to handle Bridezilla." He stepped back out of my space and grabbed the wineglasses. "But I shouldn't have threatened to take away the job offer if you couldn't get here." Well, yes, that part was a dick move. "So, balcony?"

"Sounds good." Maybe the crisp ocean air would help to cool my now heated body back to normal.

For the first ten minutes we filled the space between bites of our pizza with small talk. I took my last bite and pushed the plate away, relaxing back in my chair and sipping my wine. I wondered if he spent a lot of time in the hotel as a kid.

"What was it like growing up here?"

He chuckled. "Fun for me. Probably a nightmare for my grandparents."

My brows pulled together as I looked over at him. "Why?"

"I was a handful." He studied me as his lips lifted. "The first couple of years I lived here, it was more stuff like hiding in the housekeepers' carts to scare them. Running up and down the hallways. Escaping my nannies. But as I got a little older, it became breaking things and outright defiance. There was a year there when Paul, our driver—the one who picked you up from the airport today—threatened more than once to quit if I didn't get my act together."

"What changed?"

He shrugged. "Overheard a heated conversation between my grandparents and realized losing Paul wouldn't only suck for me—because he was one of my favorite people—but it would cause unnecessary stress on my grandmother. So I tried harder not to be such a dick."

I brought my wineglass to my mouth, hiding a smirk behind the rim. "How's that going for you?"

"You're here, aren't you?"

I narrowed my eyes at him. "Because I really want this job, not because you weren't a dick."

"Either way, it worked out in my favor."

He was ridiculous. The way he casually shrugged his shoulders and the easy twitch of his lips told me he owned the title of asshole often. It wasn't surprising I found him attractive. I'd dated enough of them to know I gravitated toward them. But there was another side of him I kept getting a sense of, and I'd be lying if I said I didn't want to get to know more.

His gaze met mine, and the old Angie would have melted into a puddle from the look he was sending my way. The new Angie was trying to be stronger and wiser and remember her worth. Although my body wasn't on the same page, it would eventually get there. Not that any of that mattered, because it wasn't like anything could happen between us anyway. He was now the owner of the hotel I worked for, and according to Google, he was rarely seen with the same girl twice.

I stood from my chair and grabbed our plates. "I'll take these in, and then I should head to bed."

He stared at me for a beat before nodding slightly. "Okay. Good night."

"Night."

Once inside the suite, I finally let out a deep breath. But once in my bed, I tossed and turned, wishing I could forget the seductive glint in his eye when he looked at me. I doubted he was attracted to me. The one thing I'd learned about asshole guys was they acted that way to get a reaction, not because they liked the girl.

Chapter Four

I REALLY WISHED I didn't find this chick so fucking attractive. She stood in front of me, rambling about the damn wedding this weekend that I couldn't give a shit about, and all I could think about was her breasts. The way they filled out her sweater. The deep V of cleavage that was showing.

"So, do you have any ideas?"

I blinked. What the hell were we talking about?

"Um..." Why did I sound like an idiot? "I'm sorry, what?"

"Did you hear anything I said?"

"No." At least I was honest. "Sorry."

She crossed her arms, and I bit the inside of my cheek to

29

stop the groan that wanted to slip out. I was pretty sure burying my face in my employee's boobs was on a strictly not allowed list somewhere.

When was the last time I'd gotten laid? Definitely before my grandmother passed away, and at least a week or more before that. Maybe that was my problem.

"Never mind," she huffed and tried to brush past me.

But my hand shot out and grasped the inside of her elbow. She stopped, looking up at me, and I didn't miss the way she shivered at my touch. I wasn't sure if that made me feel better or worse about being this attracted to her. Her skin felt warm under my touch, and all the blood in my body shot south. Soon she was going to realize exactly why I was distracted.

I released her. "Sorry, let's start over." It was early and the hotel's restaurant wasn't even open yet. She and I stood behind the bar. Apparently, there were two issues she needed to talk to me about. "Tell me what you need me to do. Preferably in as few words as possible. I do better with short and concise information rather than long-winded details I don't care about."

Her eyes narrowed like that made her mad, but after a moment, she sighed. "Do you know any DJs?"

"Yes."

"Can you ask around and see if you know any that are available tomorrow? The one who was supposed to be here got in a car accident and the bride is freaking out."

I nodded. "Yup. I can do that. Now what was the second issue?"

She waved me off. "I can talk with Jenny when she gets in. I'll let you know if we can't solve the problem."

"Perfect." Between Angie and Jenny, my restaurant manager, I had no doubt they'd figure it out. "See? We're making a good team."

Her brow raised, but no snarky rebuttal came from her. I almost felt disappointed. I liked her sass. A little too much, if I was honest. She was like the girls I tried my hardest to stay away from.

Women who weren't afraid to call me out for being a dick or for my playboy status usually wanted more than I was willing to give. I wasn't immune to the label I'd been given. Instead, I owned it. I made it clear that I enjoyed women for a night. Not any longer. I had no interest in a serious relationship. That came with expectations I was sure I'd never be able to meet.

But I couldn't avoid *her*, because she was now my employee.

"And you're gone again." Angie rolled her eyes.

And this was one of those expectations. Women wanted to talk, and they wanted their men to listen. Something I'd been told by many women I sucked at. Paying attention was something even my teachers and my grandmother said I struggled with growing up. It didn't matter if I was deep in thought about what they were saying, I could still miss entire chunks of conversation.

"Sorry."

She waved me off. "It's fine. My sister is like that. My brother sometimes too. I'm used to it." She smiled. "I'll try to use smaller words."

There it was. Her snark was probably going to be the death of me. Admittedly, I expected her to be annoyed. Instead, she was teasing me. She was so different from other women, and I didn't know what to make of that. Twenty-four hours ago, I'd pegged her as high maintenance. Now, I was sure that didn't fit.

"I'll go make some calls and I'll check back in with you later."

She nodded, and I headed back through the lobby to my office. But maybe what I needed was to head back to my room to take a cold shower or jerk off. I hadn't decided which yet because one would involve either having dirty thoughts about her and the other would involve trying not to have dirty thoughts. Neither seemed acceptable.

So, instead, I would work on finding her a DJ, and I'd remind myself of all the reasons I wasn't allowed to be attracted to her.

Thankfully, the connections I had on social media and in the entertainment world allowed me to solve the problem she'd tasked me with in less than an hour. Which was fine, but why the fuck did I feel so excited about it? Like a damn dog looking for a treat for going outside and pissing in the grass. Typically, I only cared about pleasing women in the bedroom, so why did this feel different?

Jesus, maybe I really did need to get laid.

At least I'd be able to solve that problem. In order to get the names of a handful of DJs from a woman I knew who did event planning, I'd gotten roped in to being her date to some work thing tomorrow night. It was a perfect win-win situation. Natalie would get to show up with a decent date on her arm, and I'd get laid. This had been our arrangement over the last year. Neither of us wanted anything serious, but we got along well enough in and out of the bedroom for our casual meetups to work out for both of us.

I found Angie sitting at a table near the bar with the bride and groom. She smiled as I approached, and my dick jumped to attention. I gritted my teeth and glanced over at the bride, hoping that would crush my growing issue.

"Hi, Mr. Reed," Angie said as I came closer. "Happy you could join us."

I had told her multiple times already to call me Wyatt, but she insisted on calling me by my last name in front of guests and other staff. I should be all for being professional, but every time she used it like that, I imagined the word *sir* tumbling from her lips as she fell to her knees in front of me.

Fuck.

I blinked and reluctantly tipped my head in her direction. "Ms. Mitchell."

A smirk pulled at her lips and mine twitched, but fire ran through my veins as I caught the groom eyeing the tits that seemed even closer to spilling out of her sweater than they had earlier in the morning. I understood far too well that Angie's curves were the stuff of every man's fantasy, but his soon-to-be wife was sitting right next to him. Shouldn't he be eyeing her tits?

Wrenching the fourth chair out—startling him and forcing his gaze to meet mine—I joined them at the table. "I solved your DJ issue."

"That's great," Angie chirped.

Both she and the bride conversed excitedly about another problem being solved. I needed to remember to ask her what the other issue was and what they'd ended up figuring out.

But currently I was still silently telling the douchebag across the table to keep his eyes on his wife and off my staff. He had the balls to lean back and cross his arms like I was barking up the wrong tree.

Look, I wasn't an angel when it came to the opposite sex, but I was always transparent. And if I even had an inkling a woman was in a serious relationship, I stayed far away. Furthermore, if I was out with someone, I wasn't checking out other women. Just because I had no interest in a serious relationship didn't mean I thought women should be disrespected.

I couldn't be happier when the couple excused themselves not ten minutes later.

"Dickhead," I muttered once they were out of earshot.

"Who?" Angie tilted her head and lines pulled between her brows.

Was she serious? No way she didn't notice him ogling her.

"The soon to-be-husband who was more interested in you than his fiancée."

33

She waved me off. "He was only being friendly."

I narrowed my eyes at her. "I didn't realize being friendly meant checking out a woman's tits. But good to know. I'll have to remember that next time I'm at the grocery store or something."

I didn't care that I was being an ass. She couldn't possibly be that naïve.

"He wasn't—" She stopped mid–head shake before glancing down at her chest. "I mean, I didn't notice, but I doubt he was looking at my boobs."

I sat back in my chair, debating how far to take this conversation. She was technically my employee. This had sexual harassment written all over it. But my curiosity got the best of me.

"What if I told you he was the second man today who'd done it?"

She scoffed. "I'd say you're delusional."

I leaned forward and folded my arms, placing them on the table. "So you can't think of any other man you talked to this morning who seemed so distracted by something he couldn't remember anything you said in the whole ten-minute conversation you had?"

She started to shake her head but froze as her eyes widened and heat flooded into her cheeks.

I relaxed back into my chair, fighting a smirk. I was dying to ask her if she knew how fucking irresistible her curves were. But I couldn't. I needed to get us back on safe ground.

"Tell me about the other problem you had."

"I...um..." She blinked once, twice, then schooled her features and sat up straight. "The champagne delivery got delayed and won't be here by tomorrow."

"Okay. I'm assuming Jenny suggested we offer prosecco instead? I know we have plenty of that on hand."

"She did."

Angie's smirk sent unease down my spine. Why did her words seem to have a *but* hanging on the end of them?

"Out with it."

"Well, Bridezilla wasn't thrilled about that solution."

"Of course she wasn't." I shrugged. "But not much we can really do. Not like we're going to offer our top-of-the-line champagne for her hundred and fifty guests."

"Right. We couldn't possibly do that. We don't even carry enough at any given time for that many people."

"Okay." I raised a brow. "What aren't you saying?"

"I offered a compromise. Jenny said you're going to be pissed, so I had to be the one to tell you."

I gritted my teeth and waited.

"I offered the champagne for the parents and the wedding party and prosecco for the rest of the guests."

I closed my eyes and counted. One, two, three...

They would need at least four bottles, maybe five. At almost five hundred a bottle. Add in the cost of the prosecco, and that would be more than triple the cost factored into the original price. But honestly, I could also understand that the mistake was on our end, and at the end of the day, we had to make it right.

"Wow, Jenny wasn't kidding. You do have a vein on your forehead that looks as if it might explode any minute."

I opened my eyes and glared at her.

"You know I made the right call. As much as it sucks, it wasn't their fault our order didn't come in time."

"Maybe." I shrugged. "I probably would have only offered the champagne for the bride and groom, not the whole wedding party and parents."

"That seems shitty, given the parents of the bride are the ones paying for it."

True. But it was done. Nothing I could do about it now.

"Hey, Wyatt?" Steven said, stepping into the bar area. "We have guests asking for a manager."

I tipped my head in Angie's direction. "Want to try your hand at a disgruntled hotel guest?"

She pushed her chair back and stood. "Sure. Can't be any worse than Bridezilla."

"Try not to give away three thousand dollars this time."

She rolled her eyes. "I'll try."

As she turned and followed Steven out of the restaurant, ass swaying, my gaze zeroed in on her and I held back the groan that rose up. Off-limits, I reminded myself.

Again.

Chapter Five

ANGIE

I TRIED to focus on the chicken and vegetables I had sautéing in the pan, but I found Wyatt's eyes on me unnerving, and I had no clue why. Maybe it had to do with him basically admitting he'd been distracted by my breasts. I wasn't sure how I felt about that. At the time, I hadn't even noticed. I wouldn't have even considered it a possibility. But now that I was aware it was not only a possibility but a reality, I couldn't seem to stop thinking about it.

"That smells delicious."

His voice pierced through my thoughts, and I glanced over my shoulder at where he leaned back on the kitchen island.

"It's just chicken and vegetables." I hadn't even added seasoning to it yet, but the onions and peppers were giving off a fragrant smell. I'd gotten better at cooking fairly healthy meals in the last year rather than eating out all the time. So I'd decided to run to the store and get a small amount of groceries to get me through the weekend.

Thinking about food had the other thing I needed to discuss with him popping into my head, especially since I had less than a week to prepare. After grabbing the fajita seasoning packet and mixing it into the ingredients in the pan, I looked back at him. "What do you have planned for Employee Appreciation Day?"

He cocked an eyebrow. "What do you mean?"

"You know, to show the staff your appreciation?"

"I pay them. Isn't that appreciation enough?"

I rolled my eyes and turned my attention back to the stovetop. "You should do a brunch or luncheon."

"Why?" He barked out a laugh. I didn't even need to see him to know he was shaking his head. "Can they not feed themselves?"

Jesus. Was he always like this? "That's not the point." I clicked off the burner and spun to face him. "Employee Appreciation Day is when the owner or managers do something nice for the staff to show their appreciation above and beyond paying them to do a job." I crossed my arms and narrowed my eyes at him. "It's one of the things your grandmother talked about, and it seemed like it was important to her. Am I wrong?"

He sighed and pushed off the island before coming to stand in front of me. "No, you're not wrong. She usually does some type of catered lunch, if I remember correctly."

For a heartbeat, I swore his gaze lowered. It was so quick and subtle I might've missed it if I wasn't paying attention. His eyes darkened, the lighter shade of green almost nonexistent, and the air around us suddenly felt charged.

I froze. He was my boss, so it didn't matter if the way he was looking at me sent tingles shooting down my spine. Again. I stepped around him, grabbing our plates with tortillas on them from the island.

"So, what do you have planned?" I asked as I turned back to him.

"Planned?" He blinked rapidly at me like my question had caught him off guard.

"Yeah, for Employee Appreciation Day."

He shook his head as a seductive chuckle left his lips. "Oh. That. Right."

What else did he think we were talking about?

He took the plates from me and shrugged. "I don't have anything planned, and I'm not sure if Nana B did or not."

"Can I ask... How'd she—" I snapped my mouth shut, seeing the immediate pain and anger in his eyes. He wasn't ready to talk about it. I could totally respect that.

"Aneurysm." The word came out clipped, like the sheer mention of it made him angry.

"I'm sorry." I was decent at reading a room and wasn't going to push. I stepped up to the stove, scooping the fajita mixture onto the first tortilla and needing to change the subject now that tension hung in the air. "I'll ask around, see if there's a place that usually caters the luncheon for Employee Appreciation Day. Weekends are usually busier times for catering, so we might not be able to get something for next Friday on such short notice, but we could do another day earlier in the week. Like Tuesday or Wednesday. Either way, I can take care of it." Maybe that was overstepping. "I mean, if you want me to."

"Yeah. Fine." He huffed. "Just don't spend a fortune."

"Wouldn't dream of it." I fought an eye roll. Even if I

thought he was being an idiot at the moment, he was still the boss.

"Balcony again?"

"Sure."

He's my boss, I chanted again and again in my head as I sensed him watching me while I finished plating the food. But when he finally stepped away, a mix of disappointment and relief flooded me, and I didn't know what to think about that.

Chapter Six

WYATT

I STOPPED dead in my tracks as I came into the kitchen. Angie's ass in tight black leggings was all I could see as she was bent over in front of the fridge.

All of this felt weird to me. I wasn't used to having women here because I never had them stay over. And although it felt strange, having Angie here was also kind of nice.

Last night after she went back inside to head to bed, I missed her presence. She didn't seem to mind silence or feel the need to fill it with small talk. I was even surprised by how quickly she dropped the conversation of how Nana B died when she saw my visceral reaction to it. I was prepared for her to push the subject or bring it back up again.

Eventually I'd have to deal with it and get over the betrayal, but every time it came up, the whole thing made me mad. My grandmother had known of her diagnosis for years and hadn't thought I needed to know.

I focused on the scene in front of me and unsuccessfully held in the groan that bubbled up and slipped out from between my lips. In a heartbeat, Angie popped up and spun, eyes wide. Her gaze drifted lower, taking in my bare chest. I liked her eyes on me. I shouldn't, but I did.

I took a step farther into the kitchen, and her big brown eyes shot to my face. Heat pooled in them and *fuck*, I'd never wanted a woman like I did in that moment. To see how she would react to my touch....

I shook my head.

I had to get laid. That had to be my issue. It had been too long, and with the stress of my grandmother dying and leaving me the hotel to run, I needed the release. A night with Natalie would solve my issues.

"Good morning," I mumbled, averting my gaze and heading to the coffee maker to set up a pot to brew.

"Good morning."

There was a seductive breathiness to her voice, and I gritted my teeth. The more time I spent with her, the more obvious it was that the attraction was mutual, and I hated it. She was the kind of girl who deserved someone who could give her every-thing. A forever type of girl. If I thought there was any chance I could give her that, I would have already acted on the attraction I felt.

I'd tried a semiserious relationship only once, and it blew up, showing me exactly where my faults were. She was quick to tell me repeatedly how selfish and inattentive I was. That I never listened to her or cared about her. I'd tried, but ultimately it wasn't enough. Even the few casual relationships I'd had ended because I wasn't invested enough and didn't care enough to make the effort.

Casual hookups that only lasted a night were the only thing I was good at. But when Angie was around, I kept forgetting that. And it pissed me off.

"I have plans tonight," I blurted out.

When she didn't respond, I stole a glance over my shoulder at her. She cocked her head, and her brows pulled together slightly.

"Just letting you know I'll be away from the hotel tonight for a few hours." I turned back to the coffee maker. "You have my number if anything major comes up. But I'll probably be back late."

"Okay." Her voice held a hint of disappointment.

Did she look forward to our dinners on the balcony? If so, that was even more reason to start drawing more lines. The last thing I wanted was to let her think there was any chance of something happening between us.

We moved around the kitchen in silence, and after pouring my coffee, I went back to my room to get ready for the day.

The wedding day, to be precise. Angie had said she would handle most of it and she'd come and get me if she needed me. Which was fine by me. She could handle wedding stuff and I'd be available for front desk and other issues.

Things started off okay. Once we were out of the suite and busy dealing with each of our tasks, the day went quickly. Until I almost stumbled and froze, spotting her hustling around inside the ballroom, helping the staff get the final touches done. The black dress she wore accented her figure in all the right places.

The smile she wore was genuine and reminded me of my grandmother. She'd always done all this with happiness, even when she was dealing with problems or complaints. I still didn't understand how. In only a week, I was already over-whelmed by it all. The business side of things came naturally to me. But the people? Not so much.

As much as I hated to admit it, maybe Nana B knew it too and brought Angie on knowing I needed someone who could handle the guests and staff the way she always had.

I blew out a breath and made my feet move. A few more hours, and I could get out of here and away from the thoughts of the beauty in the black dress plaguing me.

Chapter Seven

ANGIE

TODAY HAD GIVEN me more fulfillment and pride in my job than anything else I'd done. It reminded me of how much I enjoy interacting with people and being busy. I'd never been good at sitting for long periods of time. Even as a kid. That was ultimately what I figured out with my computer major in college. Sitting for hours in front of a computer didn't do it for me. It was boring and didn't keep my mind or body busy enough.

I had enjoyed my waitressing job and, most recently, the management position. The pace of a restaurant, meeting and talking with new people, was perfect for keeping me busy and happy. That was probably why the idea of some place new had excited me so much.

I exited the ballroom and headed toward the front lobby. The wedding had run smoothly. Little to no issues, thankfully. The staff was still cleaning up and getting ready to start breaking down, waiting for the last of the guests to leave. But worry shot through me as I looked up and found Steven approaching.

"Angie?"

"What do you need?" I could tell from his facial expression he didn't like what he had to ask me.

"Um." He shifted on his feet. "I called Drake over at the fire department to come assist us with an issue but wanted to give you a heads-up."

"Is there a fire?"

He shook his head. "No." A blush crept up his neck and into his face. "A couple decided to use handcuffs for, um, fun."

Oh my. I couldn't help but chuckle. But poor Steven looked so uncomfortable.

"Apparently they can't find the key."

I barked out a laugh. "Okay. When the firefighter gets here, can you bring him in through the side entrance? We don't want to alarm any of the guests."

He nodded. "Yeah, that's what I was thinking."

Once Steven walked away, my gaze landed on Wyatt as he walked through the lobby with his arm draped around a woman. A tall, gorgeous woman with a trim waist and thighs that probably didn't rub together when she walked. And I bet she didn't need to wear Spanx under the dress that seemed two sizes too small for her. It fit that tight. I could never get away with anything like that. Even with Spanx pulling everything in, I would never feel comfortable in a dress that snug.

She was the plans he had tonight. God, I felt like an idiot. There had been a few times when I thought he was looking at me like he wanted me. This little display made it obvious to me I was nowhere near his type. Which was fine. I was his employee. Nothing more.

He tipped his head in my direction, and I narrowed my eyes. His smirk told me he knew he was getting a rise out of me and enjoying it. Asshole.

I wouldn't give him the pleasure and yanked my gaze away from the two of them, focusing back on what I was doing. But as time ticked by, I became increasingly angrier with myself.

Why did I not look for somewhere else to stay? Now I had to share a room with the playboy and his revolving door of women. Would I have to witness or hear them going at it? The simple thought made me want to throw up. Maybe I could sleep on one of the sofas in the lobby.

Blanche was such a sweet woman. How she was the grandmother of such a jerk, I couldn't understand. I blew out a harsh breath. Was I being unreasonably angry? It wasn't his fault my pride was hurt because I'd started to read into things that weren't there.

I turned around and headed back to the ballroom to check on the staff and to assist so I could finally sit and relax with a glass of prosecco.

After making sure I wasn't needed in the ballroom, I ran into Steven and his friend Drake. Thankfully, they were able to handle our guests' situation without any fuss. I chuckled, thinking of how shocked I was when Drake spoke, and a thick British accent came out. He was tall and muscular, and I wasn't expecting him to be British.

My feet ached as I finally made my way to the bar. The bartender poured me a glass from the opened bottle of prosecco from the wedding.

"Thanks, Bryan."

He nodded, and I kicked off my heels. With the shoes dangling in one hand and my glass in the other, I made my way out to the pool area and sat in one of the loungers. Happiness spread through me as I listened to the waves, smelling the salty air as the tide came and taking in the lighthouse illuminated by the bright light of the moon. I could sit out here all night. The water calmed me.

Movement from the door that led from the lobby to the pool area caught my eye. What the hell was he doing out here? And where was the girl he was with earlier?

His eyes found mine, and the smile he sent me made my stomach flip.

Stop it, Angie. He was just with another woman, I reminded myself.

I swallowed thickly as he sauntered over and sat in the chair next to me.

"Refill?" He held up a bottle of the expensive champagne we'd given the bridal party.

I stare at him wide-eyed. Had he lost his mind? "From the five-hundred-dollar champagne?"

"Is that not what you're drinking?" He tipped his head at the flute in my head.

My mouth fell open. "No. It's the prosecco."

"Well, now you need to try this." A smirk lifted his lips as he reached for my glass. "It's like sex in a glass."

I rolled my eyes.

"Everything go okay after I left?" He handed me the champagne he'd poured.

"Yep." I took a sip, and a moan bubbled up, slipping through my lips. Jesus, he was right. It was like an orgasm in my mouth.

I peered over at him, and a heated stare looked back at me. I ran my tongue along my upper lip, tasting the champagne all over again and letting out another moan. Desire pooled in my belly as he tracked my movements, his pupils blowing out more as each second passed.

What was I doing? It didn't matter how he was looking at me. He'd literally just had sex with someone else.

I cringed at the reminder. "What happened to your lady friend?"

"What are you, my grandmother?" he scoffed. "Who says lady friend?"

With a shrug, I focused back on the water. "Just trying to be polite."

"Polite?"

"Fuck buddy would be rude." I attempted to mask the emotions behind my words.

"Jealous?"

Not well enough, apparently. I jerked my gaze back to him and froze. He leaned forward intently, forearms braced on his knees and a seductive smirk that left me breathless.

Absolutely not hung on the tip of my tongue, but for the life of me, I couldn't force it past my lips.

Chapter Eight

WYATT

WHAT THE FUCK was I doing? Or rather, what was wrong with me?

When I was upstairs, the desire to be with Natalie, to solve what I thought was my problem, was nonexistent. But now I wanted Angie to admit she was jealous? Of what? Because nothing even happened. Maybe Natalie was right, and I needed to figure out what was going on and what I wanted.

Usually, I wanted easy. But at the event, when Natalie barely interacted with me other than to introduce people, I got increasingly annoyed. Then when we were in the elevator heading up to my room, I tried to engage her in conversation only to have her spend fifteen minutes telling me about her recent experience buying a pair of shoes.

I was done, to say the least.

Angie studied me, and *asshole* flashed through my mind. Because it didn't matter that I wanted so desperately to lift her dress and bury my face between her legs until she screamed my name. And it didn't matter if she was jealous. Because she was a forever type of girl. I couldn't give her that, so I had to stop this game I was playing.

"I got rid of her." I shrugged and sat back in the lounger, focusing my gaze on the water. "She was too talkative." I took a large swig of my champagne.

No way was I going to admit what actually happened. That for the first time in years, I had no interest in a beautiful woman. And I sure as hell wasn't telling her that all I kept thinking about was the look of disgust Angie sent me when I walked into the hotel with Natalie. It was better if I owned the role of playboy.

"That's so nice of you." I caught her eye roll in my periphery.

Why her opinion of my personal life mattered, I didn't know. It had only been three days, but she was already getting under my skin. If I was honest, she'd gotten under my skin before she even showed up on Thursday. But now in a totally different way. Almost obsessive. All I could think about was getting back down here to see how her day had gone.

"The employee appreciation luncheon is scheduled for Tuesday," Angie said after minutes of silence.

"Great." I needed to remember to do something for Angie. Between arriving early to deal with the wedding and scheduling the luncheon, she really had been an asset in the last couple of days. My grandmother always found doing special things for the staff and our guests important, even though I thought it was a waste of money.

"And I'm going to go to the florist shop in town sometime this week to replace the flowers in the lobby."

"Why?" I tilted my head and studied her. "I thought we only had those for the wedding?"

Angie's brows pulled together. "Didn't your grandmother always have flower arrangements in the lobby?"

"Not sure. I never really paid attention."

"Maybe you should."

And there it was. The reminder that I wasn't good at that stuff. It was why my grandmother knew I would need someone who was. I narrowed my eyes.

"Just saying." Her shoulders lifted and fell, her gaze softening slightly. "Maybe you should try to notice the little details around this hotel that make it so special. Like flowers in the lobby. When I first came here for my interview and saw the beautiful display of flowers that were scattered around the lobby, it made me smile. I immediately loved the place. And the lights outside that were strung up and spanned the length of the wraparound porch. The throw pillows on the sofas and chairs and the paintings hanging on the walls. All of that adds a special charm to the place that other places don't have. You know?"

"You're telling me flowers and throw pillows are making our guests happy?" I wasn't sure I would ever understand that, but I wanted to try. *She* made me want to see things the way she saw them.

"Yes." She chuckled. "In the fewest number of words, that's what I'm telling you."

"You sound like my grandmother." I shook my head and sat forward, grabbing the bottle of champagne and topping off our glasses. "You're as nuts as she was."

"Or maybe we have an eye for these things and you don't."

"I don't think we need to spend any more of the hotel's profits on stupid crap like throw pillows and flowers. That's not what makes us money."

"I think you're wrong. Blanche ran this hotel for more than forty years and built it into what it is now. You should have a little more faith in what she thought was best."

Now I felt like a kid being reprimanded. What was I going to say to that? *No. I don't want to preserve my grandmother's memory or do any of the things she found important?*

Jesus.

"Fine. Whatever." Flowers and throw pillows. Why not? Let's throw more money away instead of trying to make money. I might lose my goddamn mind.

She shifted in the lounger next to me, and her dress rode up her thighs. Blood shot south as I took in the creamy expanse of skin above her knees. I wanted to reach out and stop her when she yanked at the hem, pulling the material back down.

The brink of insanity felt even closer as I subtly adjusted myself. Her breath hitched. I didn't want to make her uncomfortable, but at the same time, part of me wanted her to know the effect she had on me. I met her wide-eyed stare, detecting both confusion and disbelief.

Words spilled from my mouth without thought. "You don't realize how fucking gorgeous you are, do you?"

Pink tinged her cheeks, and her gaze lowered to her dress. "Please don't. I know I'm bigger than most women. Especially the ones you seem to date."

I gritted my teeth. "Jesus, Angie. I wish I could show you exactly what I think of your body."

A whisper of a scoff came from her, and it only egged me on.

"I'm sitting here talking with you, hard as a rock, whereas an hour ago, I couldn't even get it up."

Her wide eyes raised to mine. "What? You didn't…"

This was such a bad idea. I needed to stop, but I shook my head. "No, Angie. All I could think about was coming back down here to talk to you."

She studied me, and I held her gaze, letting her see whatever she needed to. I knew nothing could happen, but I'd be damned if I'd let her believe I didn't want something to.

Chapter Nine

ANGIE

I DIDN'T KNOW what to think. Why was he saying all this? Did I believe he hadn't slept with the beautiful woman he'd taken up to his room earlier? Why would he lie about that? Better question: Why did I care?

"Wyatt?" Steven's voice broke through the moment.

"Yeah?" Wyatt groaned and glanced over at where the young guy stood, holding the door open.

Relief flooded me. I refused to get attached to the idea that Wyatt was attracted to me.

"We have a problem." Steven looked back and forth between Wyatt and me. "Might need both of you."

We followed him inside to the lobby. A young girl, not much older than four or five, sat curled up on a chair with a stuffed bear.

"She showed up in the lobby about five minutes ago." Steven glanced our way. "I've been trying to get her to tell me where she came from, but she won't talk."

Wyatt moved toward her before I could even utter a word. He sat on the corner of the long accent table in front of the chair, and immediately, the little girl held up her bear, showing it to him.

"Well, I'll be..." Steven shook his head. "She acted scared of me. Surprisingly likes you, though."

Wyatt smiled back at us. "What do you mean surprisingly? I'm good with kids."

I shook my head, mirroring Steven's surprise. The man who didn't like dealing with people was good with kids.

"I'm going to start calling guests that had children on their reservation." I eyed Wyatt as he interacted with the young child. "Can you see if you can get her to talk?"

"I'll do my best." He shrugged, directing his next words to Steven. "Can you get coloring paper and a set of crayons from the restaurant?"

"Yep."

I headed toward the front desk as Steven made his way to the restaurant. As I stood there, calling guests, my gaze kept seeking out Wyatt as he sat on the floor coloring with the young girl. He had her smiling after the first few calls I made and was more comfortable with the small girl than even I would have been. It seemed so out of character. But then again, I barely knew him. He really could be good with kids.

I'd half expected him to tell Steven and me to deal with it. I shook my head. This guy was a walking contradiction, that was for sure.

Before I could call the next guest, a young woman in one of

our housekeeping uniforms appeared, frantically looking around the lobby before her gaze zeroed in on Wyatt and the girl.

"Oh, thank God." She beelined straight for her and scooped her up. "Chelsea, I told you not to wander off."

I stepped out and walked over.

The woman bowed her head, refusing to meet either one of our eyes. "I'm so sorry. My babysitter canceled and I didn't have a choice but to bring her."

Wyatt stood, eyeing the young woman. "Sadie, why didn't you say something? We would have understood if you needed to take off."

The woman's head popped up and her eyes widened. "No, sir. I couldn't."

"What do you mean?"

I was pretty sure I understood, and it wasn't something I thought Wyatt would, though.

"I can't afford to take any time off." She averted her gaze again. "And with Chelsea being so sick this winter, I've burned through all my paid leave."

Jesus, that sucked. It was only March. I made a mental note to look into it. Was she new or had she been here for a while? I wanted to get familiar with all the staff and their situations, but that would come with time. It surprised me that Wyatt knew this woman by name. Was he familiar with all the staff?

Wyatt looked from the little girl and back to her mother. "How much longer do you have on your shift?"

"An hour or so."

Wyatt nodded. "Okay. We can sit with Chelsea while you finish up."

"That's not necessary—"

"It'll be easier for you, and I don't mind. And if you want to leave a little early, that's fine too."

Was he serious? Occupying the kid for a few minutes was

one thing, but to sit with her for another hour? Nothing in his expression said otherwise.

Sadie hesitated, obviously unsure of what to do.

"I'll come get you if Chelsea needs you," I added, to make her feel more comfortable. My parents had worked long hours, leaving my younger sister and me with our older brother a lot, just to make ends meet, so I understood where she was coming from. I was still surprised Wyatt understood her situation.

Again, walking contradiction... but... Thinking about his interactions with the staff over the last three days, it was apparent he cared. Asking the maintenance guy how his wife was doing, leaving pizza in the staff lounge, talking to Jenny about her college classes. Maybe he wasn't good at dealing with people's complaints and demands, like Bridezilla. Or noticing the flowers that littered the lobby. But he obviously didn't lack empathy, and he made it a point to know his staff.

"Okay." She set the little girl back down. "I'll finish cleaning the ballroom and then I'll probably head out early."

Wyatt nodded. "That works."

After ten minutes of coloring, two rounds of hide and seek, and five rounds of I spy, Sadie reappeared, thanking us and gathering her daughter before heading out.

To say I was exhausted was an understatement. "I don't know if I want to soak in a hot bath or climb into bed."

"You go ahead." He waved toward the elevators. "I'll check in with the night shift."

"You sure?"

"Yes." His gaze heated my body as it trailed its way down. "Use the en suite attached to my room. It has a large soaking tub."

The thought of being in his personal space was doing weird things to me. I wasn't sure if it was making me nervous or excited or both.

God, I was ridiculous. I straightened my back and crossed

my arms under my breasts, feeling confident when his gaze locked on my cleavage. I shouldn't be allowing his attention or encouraging it. But we both knew there was a line we couldn't cross, so what was the harm?

Finally, his eyes met mine, heat swirling there, and I puckered my lips in a seductive pout. My breath hitched as he crowded my space and leaned down. His mouth inches from my ear caused gooseflesh to pebble along my skin.

"I like seductive, playful Angie."

His warm breath along my skin sent desire coursing through me. I squeezed my legs together to ease the tension.

"And if I thought I could give you what you deserve, I wouldn't hesitate to give us both what we want."

Before I could even ask what he meant, he was gone, walking toward the front desk, and leaving me there like a puddle of goo on the floor.

Chapter Ten

WYATT

I SLID my keycard through the slot and pushed the door to my suite open. Thoughts of Angie naked, soaking in my Jacuzzi tub, had consumed me since she'd walked away. Nothing could happen, but that didn't stop me from fantasizing about it.

Disappointment flooded me as I took in the quiet suite and the closed door that led to her room. She'd probably gone to bed already. What was I doing? Did I think she would be waiting for me? Jesus. I'd made it clear I wasn't giving her anything she deserved. I doubted she wanted a quick fuck with her new boss.

Utter fucking asshole. That was for sure.

But the minute I stepped into my room, my gaze landed on the closed bathroom door and the dim light visible under the door. Images of her naked in the tub flooded me, and my dick pushed against the zipper of my pants, demanding to be freed.

Not going to happen. He needed to chill the fuck out.

I pushed my suit jacket off, throwing it onto the bed, and then yanked at the knot of my tie. I worked the buttons of my dress shirt open and pulled the shirt from the waistband of my pants.

Rustling came from the other side of the door, and when it swung open, I was met with a vision of Angie wrapped in a towel. One of *my* large bath towels that hugged her luscious curves tightly and was anchored together in the middle of her breasts.

Why had I thought this was a good idea? I couldn't even think straight as I stared at her, sure that there was no blood left in my top head because it had all been redirected to my lower one.

She was so fucking beautiful. Blond hair piled high on her head. Dark eyes lined by wet lashes. Lips pink and plump. I trailed my gaze lower. Her round, full tits were ready to pop out of the top of the towel, and the strong scent of honeysuckle drifted toward me.

"Sorry." She shifted, and as her gaze trailed down my chest and abs, her teeth pressing into her lower lip.

I loved feeling her eyes on me. Drinking me in like I was her. The towel she wore was the last barrier between me and the body I craved more than anything else I'd ever wanted.

"I'll get out of your space." She shifted again. "Thank you for letting me use your tub."

I couldn't speak. I just stood frozen, staring at her.

"Wyatt?" She took a step closer. "You okay?"

She was inches away, and I stole another glance down at her inviting breasts. Without permission, my hand snaked out, latching on to her waist. Her breath hitched as I pulled her close to my body.

When she moved her hands from her towel and placed them on my chest, my grip tightened on her waist and my hard cock pressed against her. *Fuck.* She felt so damn perfect like this. So right.

Her mouth fell open as she tilted her head back to look up at me. I wanted this moment with her. Just a moment. I couldn't have more than that.

The feel of her hands on my skin branded me, and every nerve ending in my body came alive.

"Wyatt." My name fell from her lips as a breathy whisper.

My subconscious screamed at me that this was a bad idea. But I found myself leaning forward, sucked in by her deep caramel-colored eyes and pink lips.

I wasn't prepared for the moment our mouths fused. The sensations it sent coursing through me. It was unlike anything I'd experienced before. Her mouth opened slightly, and I tilted my head, thrusting my tongue inside and deepening the kiss. Our tongues dueled in desperation. I walked her backward until I had her pinned to the wall with my body, my thigh wedged between her legs.

I felt the warmth and wetness of her pussy through my pants, reminding me she was in only a towel. She rubbed herself against my thigh and trailed her fingers up my chest, disappearing under my shirt, and I sensed the towel under my touch come loose. If I let it fall to the floor, she would be standing in front of me completely naked and ready for my mouth. My touch. My cock.

Exactly what I wanted. But also nothing I was allowed to have. She wasn't only my employee, but a woman who would not only expect more, but deserved more.

I held tightly to the towel at her sides and broke the kiss. "We can't do this," I gritted out.

Her eyes popped open, and she searched my face before anger flashed through her gaze. She pushed at my chest and grabbed the towel where it had come loose between her breasts. "A little late for that, don't you think?"

She didn't even give me a chance to explain before she was storming away. I forced myself to keep my feet planted. Following her and trying to explain wouldn't help the situation. I'd fucked up. Given into my attraction even when I knew nothing could happen between us. She had every right to be pissed at me.

I flinched when I heard her door slam. Finally, I moved, stomping into the bathroom and turning on the shower.

The cold shower without any relief was the punishment I deserved for taking things too far. But even the chilly water did nothing to lessen my problem, and I found myself fisting my cock anyway. Images of storming into her room, bending her over the edge of her bed, and plowing into her over and over flashed through my mind as I moved my hand up and down my shaft.

"Son of a bitch," I bit out, letting go and slamming both hands against the wall.

No. I wouldn't give myself the release after what I'd done. The only silver lining was that her anger would surely put some distance between us. Or she might decide to quit and head back to North Carolina.

That thought sent my gut plummeting.

Chapter Eleven

ANGIE

I DID NOT WANT to see Wyatt, but I was not about to let what happened the night before stop me from doing my job either. I refused to give this up over some playboy who couldn't keep it in his pants and thought he was God's gift to women.

To be honest, I was madder at myself for letting him affect me the way he did than I was at his actions. I should've known better. But I wouldn't let it happen again. That was for damn sure.

I stomped through the suite and headed into the kitchen to start coffee. My feet stuck to the floor as I froze when a note on the center island caught my eye. I hesitated. Did I care what he had to say?

Who was I kidding? Of course I cared. It's why I was still so angry—because a large part of me really thought there was something between us. More than only mutual attraction. That I affected him just as much as he did me. When he gripped the towel, I was so close to jumping into bed with him and possibly ruining how hard I'd worked to get here. I'd never done anything so stupid in my life, especially because of a guy. I wanted so badly to hear that he felt this thing between us too. But I wasn't naïve enough to believe that was what the note said. I could only hope.

After taking a calming breath, I stepped closer and picked up the paper.

I'M SO sorry about last night. Nothing I can say would justify my actions. I shouldn't have crossed that line with you knowing I'm only good for a night. I don't do relationships, and letting anything happen between us like I did last night wasn't fair to you. I can't apologize enough.

You're my employee, and that was another line I should have never crossed. In just three days, you've impressed me. I can see now why my grandmother hired you. I understand if you decide you can't stay, but I'm hoping that isn't the case. I left early this morning for Boston. I think that's for the best for the time being. I'll be back on Wednesday. Steven knows to call me if anything comes up that needs my attention.

-Wyatt

With my breath still lodged in my throat, I skimmed over the note again. I had so many conflicting emotions.

I appreciated his honesty, but I wished he would have waited and said all of this to me.

Maybe he wasn't sure I'd listen. I'd stormed off after he

pulled away. Did the fact that he let his guard down enough to kiss me mean he felt this insane connection between us too? Or was I reading into things that weren't there?

I didn't know what to make of any of it. At least I had a couple of days to get my thoughts and feelings in line before I had to see him again. And to figure out where I was going to stay, because, obviously, staying in this suite with him was no longer an option.

The day went quickly, and by early afternoon, the wedding guests had all left. I tried not to think about Wyatt and the way I'd felt when he kissed me. The way he'd made me feel sexy and desired, something I wasn't used to. I was struggling to understand why he'd kissed me if he had no intentions of letting it go farther.

Why did he believe he was only good for a night? Granted, I didn't really know him, but in just a few days, he'd made me feel more worthy than any man ever had. He seemed kind, giving, and observant to small details like what I was drinking and that I enjoyed sitting out on the balcony. Maybe he struggled to be faithful. Although that idea didn't sit right, either. He was so appalled at the thought of the groom checking out my breasts on Friday.

By the time I stepped back into the suite after a full day on my feet, I wished he was here to sit on the balcony with me and eat like we had the first two nights.

With my carry-out food from downstairs in my hand, I made my way out on the balcony. Between bites, I worried my bottom lip between my teeth and glanced at my phone before finally setting my fork down and picking it up. I pulled up Wyatt's number and typed out a message.

ME: Got your note.

. . .

THREE DOTS APPEARED IMMEDIATELY and disappeared. I waited, holding my breath until the three dots showed again and a message popped up.

WYATT: Good.

I SIGHED AND TRIED AGAIN. To the point, I reminded myself.

ME: You didn't have to leave.

Wyatt: Yes, I did.

Me: Why?

Wyatt: Obviously I can't be trusted to keep my distance from you. So the only thing I could think of was putting miles between us.

Me: That's ridiculous.

Wyatt: I agree. I should have better self-control.

Me: *eye roll* Not what I meant.

Me: We have to eventually learn to work together, so your solution is only a Band-Aid.

Wyatt: I never planned to live in Starlight Bay. Boston has been my home since college. In a couple of weeks, when you've moved into your apartment and feel comfortable, I'll run the business side of things from here while you manage the daily stuff there.

WAIT, what? My shoulders sank as a mixture of sadness and anger hit me. Although I had no right to be either. He'd made it clear he didn't want anything other than a professional relationship. I needed to respect that.

I looked down as another message came through.

WYATT: Please stay in the suite until your apartment is ready. I only plan on being there a day or two in the coming weeks and I have no issue staying in a regular room.

Me: I'm not kicking you out of your place.

Wyatt: 1. You're not. I offered.

Wyatt: 2. You need the space more than I do.

Wyatt: 3. It's the least I can do after making you start the job early and then crossing the line with you.

Me: Jesus. Martyr much?

Me: You realize I didn't try to stop you, right?

Me: I'm just as much to blame. Did you miss the fact that I was eager and willing???

Me: I probably would have let you fuck me if you hadn't stopped it.

Wyatt: Angie. Please.

Me: Please what?

Me: Don't tell the truth?

Me: Fine. I'll lie if that's what you want.

Me: You're a horrible kisser. Worst I've ever had. My pussy didn't throb and drip for you. I hated it. You're the biggest asshole. Greedy, mean. A total rake.

I SLAMMED my phone down on the table. What an idiot. Somehow that didn't change the fact that I wished he was here.

After my last text was met with silence, I decided to head to bed. Not sure what I thought my outburst would achieve. But God, he made me mad with the martyr shit he was hung up on.

But with the list of things I had to take care of tomorrow, stressing about my idiot boss couldn't be one of them.

Chapter Twelve

ANGIE

Blooms was the cutest little shop I'd ever seen. I breathed in the sweet smells of the flowers as I walked around. There was a woman helping a man looking to get flowers for his wife. With how knowledgeable the woman sounded, I assumed she was the owner.

It didn't take long for her to finish up and send the guy walking out the door with a love-filled smile on his face.

"Hi. Can I help you?" she said as she came out from behind the counter.

"Yeah. I'm Angie Mitchell."

She tilted her head, studying my face.

"I'm the new hotel manager at Charming Tides."

"Oh. Yes." She beamed. "Blanche told me she hired someone to run the place."

"It's a shame she's not here to learn from. I was really impressed when I interviewed with her."

"Yeah, we were all shocked by her death." She glanced around at the flowers before refocusing back on me. "But I can definitely help you. I've been helping Blanche with flower arrangements for the hotel for many years."

"Okay, I need some for the lobby as well as an employee luncheon we're having tomorrow."

I listened intently as she made her suggestions. I agreed we needed bright colors to match the palette of the lobby and mild scents for the tables in the staff lounge. After inquiring about what calming scents she would suggest for the hotel check-in desk, her face lit up with a smile.

"I can see now why Blanche said you were going to be perfect."

I couldn't stop the chuckle that escaped through my lips. "She kept saying that to me too, but I don't really know why."

"Because that place needs a creative, detailed touch. Someone who will continue to keep the heart that Blanche put into it. And just listening to you talk, I can see how she recognized the passion she'd been hoping for."

I followed her to the register as she took a few notes for the order. "I'll give you the invoice now to pass along to Wyatt, and I can deliver all the flowers tomorrow morning if that works."

"That's perfect."

After leaving the flower shop, I made a quick stop at Lil's Sweet Treats to grab one of their amazing handmade chocolate platters and a box of chocolate almond bark for myself. I'd earned it after all the walking I'd done. The temperature was at least mild for March, but eventually I did need to get my car from back home.

I pushed through the door of the hotel and made my way to Wyatt's office. I'd stash the chocolates in there until the luncheon. At least I knew no one would get into them.

I came out and found Steven behind the check-in counter. He picked up an envelope and handed it to me.

"What's this?" I asked, turning it over.

"It's from Wyatt."

If it was another letter, I might scream. And poor Steven didn't need that, so I stepped away to open it.

What the heck? It wasn't a letter. It was a gift certificate to the spa in town. For an outrageous amount too. At the bottom was a note.

TAKE WEDNESDAY OFF. Made you an appointment at 11a.m.

I'D HAD tons of shitty boyfriends. Bosses too. None of them would have ever thought to give me a gift card to a spa. Shaking my head, I put the paper back in the envelope and pulled out my phone.

ME: Thank you for the gift, but I can't accept it. You need to let this go. I don't need an "I'm sorry for kissing you" gift.

Wyatt: It's for Employee Appreciation Day. Since you organized the luncheon, I wanted to do something else special for you.

Wyatt: Also, to be clear... I don't regret kissing you. I'm sorry I can't be everything you want or deserve. There's a difference.

My cheeks heated, and I wanted so badly to ask him why he

thought he couldn't be everything I wanted and deserved. But I wasn't doing that through text.

Me: Thank you for the gift. If I thought you'd listen, I'd tell you all the ways you're so much more than what you think you are.

Me: And I don't regret kissing you either.

Chapter Thirteen

WYATT

ALL OF THIS would be so much easier if she would just call me an asshole and tell me she hated our kiss. In a way I believed, not with her snarky, sarcastic mouth. With plump, pink lips. So soft. So kissable. Lips that I couldn't stop imagining being wrapped around my cock as I fucked her mouth.

Damn it. Why, for Christ's sake, could I not stop thinking about her? In less than five days, she had me questioning everything I thought I'd never want.

Maybe my grandmother's words would give me insight. She was always good at that.

Slamming my phone down, I stared at the envelopes sitting

on the table in my living room in Boston. My name was written on the front of them in my grandmother's sprawling handwriting. I'd officially put off reading these for longer than I should have. But I was so mad at her after she died that I couldn't bring myself to open them. Now that I'd had some time to process, I needed to rip the Band-Aid off.

I tore open the most recent envelope and pulled out the sheet of paper. My hand shook at the sight of my grandmother's words. It had me wondering if I really was ready. Too late for that thought, I supposed.

WYATT,

If you're reading this, it must mean I have left earth and gone to be with your pop. I know you're probably mad at me for not telling you about my diagnosis. But at my age, the surgery would have been too risky, so I opted for a temporary fix that would buy me a couple more years. If I would have told you, you would have stressed and watched me like a hawk. I decided it was better if I just kept it to myself and enjoyed our time together. I trusted in the fact that when it was my time, I would get to join the love of my life in heaven.

I've been writing these letters every few months since my diagnosis. I want my words to mean something when I go.

Today I found the woman who will take my place running the hotel. Not the business side of things that you help me with. But the small things. The things that make this hotel so special. You have so many wonderful qualities, my sweet boy, but slowing down and seeing the little things isn't one of them. You have always gone full speed ahead. As a child, you ran without looking back. You jumped headfirst. As a teenager, you tested every boundary there was. No one could keep up with you. But your heart is bigger than that of anyone I've ever known. And one day, I have faith you'll see what all of us who have loved you see.

As an adult, you have lived freely and accomplished so much. But you've also closed yourself off to love. Don't think I don't know. You see the only serious relationship you've had as a failure, and you hate failure. So you have chosen to never try again. But you are older now, more mature. Not the twenty-two-year-old boy trying to impress the girl. My hope for you is that you find someone and have the type of love I had with your pop.

I am writing a stipulation in my will that you may or may not know about yet. I want you to give Angie a chance. If I know you as well as I think I do, I believe you will see just how perfect she is too. In ways that might surprise you.

With lots of love,
Nana

SHE WASN'T wrong about Angie. The woman surprised me more every day. Not only was she willing to call me out on my shit, but part of me expected her to make what happened on Saturday night a bigger deal. I saw the hurt on her face when I pulled back. She had the opportunity to milk the situation, yet she hadn't. Instead, she'd called me a fucking martyr.

At the end of the day, it was my fault. I'd always been honest with the women I slept with, and the fact that I kissed her, then almost let it go farther knowing I wouldn't be able to give her anything more, turned my stomach every time I thought about it. It wasn't like me. Even more surprising? I'd never had an issue with control when it came to my attraction to women. But, somehow, Angie made me lose my mind.

I picked up my phone and texted Paul, letting him know I'd be down in a minute. My grandmother had employed him since I was a kid, and since her death, he'd become my personal driver, even when I insisted I could drive myself. I wasn't sure if I wanted to know the answer, but I couldn't help but wonder if he'd known about Nana B's abdominal aortic aneurysm.

After she died, I had a lot of questions. Her doctor told me she had a procedure done when they first found the triple A. But it wasn't a permanent fix. She knew the graft would eventually break down and the aneurysm could rupture.

It took me a bit to come to terms with her hiding it from me. But I did understand. She and I were very similar in a lot of ways, and I would hate for people to worry and walk on eggshells around me, so I likely would have made the same decision.

I collected my stuff for the meeting and headed downstairs to find Paul waiting for me. His eyes widened when I opened the passenger side door to the black SUV and climbed in. If we were going to talk about my grandmother's diagnosis—that ultimately led to her death—I didn't want to be in the back. I wanted to be able to look at him.

"Wyatt?" His voice held a bit of uncertainty.

"Did you know?" I preferred the direct approach to hard conversations, and Paul was used to it.

He sighed and pulled out into traffic. "About Blanche's diagnosis?"

"Yeah."

He nodded. "She stopped driving entirely after she found out. She rarely got behind the wheel anymore anyway, but the fact that she stopped completely made me curious. I finally asked why, and she told me."

I gritted my teeth, trying hard not to be mad. But, Jesus, how many other people knew?

"Did you start reading the letters?" He glanced over at me.

"Yeah. Just the most recent one that she wrote after hiring Angie."

"That young woman is a firecracker." Paul smiled. "I can see why Blanche thought she was so perfect for you."

"You mean for the hotel." I looked over at him, correcting his choice of words.

He shook his head. "Nope. I meant exactly what I said. Your grandmother was convinced she's the perfect woman for you." A chuckle passed through his lips. "I didn't understand it until I picked her up from the airport last week."

I opened my mouth and then shut it again. My grandmother had hired Angie because she thought she was, what, my future wife? I shook my head. Jesus.

"She spent the first ten minutes of the drive ripping you a new one to her sister on the phone. And when she told her she planned to make it clear she wasn't going to jump every time you snapped your fingers, I was sold. You need a swift kick in the ass most days."

"Thanks," I mumbled. "But Nana B was wrong. I'm not starting a relationship with Angie. I get it. My grandparents had one of those perfect marriages—"

"Whoa, hold up." His brows furrowed. "Their marriage was anything but perfect. I think they made it look easy some days because they loved each other and worked at it. But that doesn't mean they didn't have their own problems."

"I don't remember them ever fighting, so I'm not sure I believe that."

"You were always too busy causing a ruckus to notice anything but your next adventure." He side-eyed me. "Not to mention, your grandparents were always good about having their disagreements in private. Or, rather, not in front of you or in the hotel. Many happened in the back seat of my car."

That wasn't entirely accurate, though, now that I thought about it. The memory of them arguing about Paul threatening to quit, and my grandmother's breakdown, was locked forever in my memory. I still didn't know whether it was her crying or my grandfather taking me out on the boat and reading me the riot act the next day that truly changed my behavior. But I definitely made an extra effort not to be such a dick to Paul after that. Funny enough, he became someone I truly valued.

"Sometimes the way we see things is not always the truth."

I sighed. I recognized his *I'm about to give you some unwarranted advice* voice. I'd heard it plenty of times over the last twenty years. But he remained silent until I couldn't take it anymore.

"Out with it. It's not like you to hold your tongue."

He chuckled. "That is true. But there's no point in telling you something you might not be ready to hear."

"I'll try my best to listen." Now that my grandparents were both gone, Paul was the only parental figure I had left, and his advice had never steered me wrong in the past.

"Don't let the failure of a relationship with the wrong woman mess up your opportunity with the right one."

"Now you sound like Nana B." I scoffed and turned to look out the window. "I'm good at giving women orgasms and buying them shit. I can't do all that other stuff they want."

"Says the guy who gave his girl a day off and sent her to the spa."

"She's not my girl." I gritted my teeth and left off the *yet* I wanted to add. Because, fuck, did I like the sound of that. "I did that for Employee Appreciation Day."

He laughed and I whipped around to look at him.

"Bullshit." He raised an eyebrow. "So, where's my spa gift card?"

Fuck. I hadn't done anything for Paul. I suck. "I think the whole thing is dumb. A day to show the employees you pay your appreciation by giving them stupid crap like a luncheon."

He snorted. "Yet you went above and beyond to give Angie a gift."

"It's different." At least I thought it was. "She's the one

organizing everything. It didn't feel right not to do something special for her. Especially after I demanded she end her vacation and start early. Then I left her to handle the wedding pretty much by herself. Then threw myself at her later that night before changing my mind."

His eyes widened comically. See? Even he thought I was an utter asshole.

I let out a harsh breath. "Do you see what I mean? I constantly screw things up."

"You're impulsive. Most of the time you realize it, but sometimes not until after the fact. I won't lie. You will probably spend a lot of time groveling and making it right." His lips lifted into a smirk. "But with the right woman, she'll be willing to forgive and won't hold it over your head."

"I know where you're going." We pulled up in front of the building where my meeting was, and Paul brought the car to a stop. "I don't blame Amanda."

"Yes, I know. But Wyatt, from the outside looking in, we all saw that girl as a gold-digging witch who you could never please unless you were dropping a shit ton of money on her. And even then, you couldn't make her happy."

If any of that were true, it made sense that she ended up marrying a rich old guy. But he obviously made her happy, so what did that say?

I pushed the car door open and stepped out, over this conversation. "I'll text when I'm done."

He nodded, and I shut the door before turning and making my way inside.

Being a board member of this charity was one of the things I took pride in. The founder was a genius, and his prototype blew my mind. He was getting reliable, easy-to-use devices in the hands of nonverbal kids who struggled to communicate. Most were still using large books that were clunky and not easy or quick to manage. These devices were next level and were already making a huge difference now that we had the charity off the ground. I wanted to invest my parents' money in things I knew they'd be proud of.

I barely remembered my mom, but according to stories my grandmother told me, she volunteered a lot in the special ed program at the local school. She also led a program at church and donated to organizations that helped fund materials and assistance in schools. So when I came across this opportunity, I knew she would approve. And so would Nana B.

But as excited as I was to be there, my mind ran in circles through the meeting. Between the texts with Angie, the letter from my grandmother, and then the conversation with Paul, I was pretty sure I heard nothing of what was said during the entire hour I was in the boardroom. Luckily, I was a pro at faking my inattention. Except with Angie, apparently.

A smirk lifted my lips as I thought about her tits that day, ready to pop free from that sweater. Then my mind drifted to her flushed skin, hair high on her head, standing in my bathroom in only a towel. One that clung tightly to her gorgeous curves.

Fuck. I blinked and shifted uncomfortably, trying unsuccessfully to focus on the meeting. Once I was downstairs and pulling open the door, I was frustrated to say the least. What the hell was it about Angie that I couldn't shake?

"What if I fail again?" I asked after climbing back into the front seat. "Because I see how Angie could be a good fit for all the shit I hate doing at the hotel. So, what if I fuck it up?" I huffed. "Then she'll be gone, and I'll be left picking up the pieces again. Dealing with bridezillas and flowers, fucking throw pillows. I'm not good at that shit. You know that."

"You realize I'm not in your head?" He pulled out into traffic and stole a glance my way. "But I don't think her quitting is what's holding you back from trying something serious with her either. If that's what you're asking."

"Of course that's what I'm fucking asking." I gritted my teeth. "Wasn't that the whole point of your lecture earlier?"

"Yes. But since when do you actually listen to me?"

I rolled my eyes. "Since I can't get her outta my head. I thought distance would help, but it's making me crazy."

When the smirk appeared on his lips, part of me wanted to punch him.

"You have it bad."

I let my head fall back against the headrest and closed my eyes. Was I really considering this? Eight years since my relationship with Amanda imploded, and I'd had zero issues with casual hookups. In only five days, Angie had gotten under my skin and made me want things I never thought I would.

"I need to grab a few things from my condo, but then I want to head back to Starlight Bay."

"Atta boy." He bumped my knee with his fist, and I glared over at him. That damn smirk of his was still there. "Another word of advice?"

"Do I have a choice?"

"Not really." He shrugged. "She might take a little convincing about your sudden change of heart."

"Yeah." I sighed. "Any ideas, old man?"

Now it was his turn to glare at me. "Start with a date, Casanova."

A date. Excitement ran through me as I imagined walking into a restaurant with her on my arm, walking around the art gallery, seeing her face light up like it did at the painting hanging in the owner's suite.

Fuck yeah. This was brilliant. Now to come up with a plan that she couldn't say no to.

Chapter Fourteen

ANGIE

I LOOKED up from the hotel's front desk when the bell above the door chimed, and my breath caught in my throat.

Wyatt.

God, he was so good looking. Tall, hair effortlessly tousled, piercing green eyes that held mine as he closed the space. He filled out his slacks and dress shirt in the sexiest of ways, especially with the top three buttons undone. I ran my tongue along my upper lip and tried to ignore the throbbing between my legs.

How he caused such a visceral reaction in me, I had no clue.

He leaned his forearms on the counter in front of me and sent me that smirk of his that really needed to come with a warning label. Because it was doing all kinds of things to my body that I didn't even want it to.

"You're back?" Oh wow. Apparently, he made me sound like an idiot too.

"I am." He leaned in closer. "Have you eaten yet?"

I glanced down at the watch on my wrist. Was it really almost six? "No, not yet."

"Good." He pushed off the counter. "I'll let Steven know we'll be off premises."

I raised a brow. What the hell was he talking about?

He studied me, that smirk still plastered on his face. "I want to show you something and then take you to dinner."

I crossed my arms under my breasts. A shiver raced down my spine as his pupils blew out when his gaze landed on my cleavage.

"Why?"

He blinked before meeting my eyes again. "Why?" he repeated.

"Yes. Why are you here? Why are you wanting to take me to dinner? Cause I swear to God, if this is another attempt at apologizing, I'm going to lose my freaking mind."

He shook his head, and for a hot second, he seemed nervous. But then the cocky smirk was back. "I want to take you on a date."

I stumbled back before catching myself. Was he serious?

"Angie." He leaned back on the counter. "No expectations. Just one date. That's all I'm asking. If, after tonight, you want nothing to do with me, we can go back to the original plan."

"Original plan?"

"Yeah. I'll run the business side from Boston, you'll manage the daily stuff here." His lips twitched. "At least until I can find a way to erase you from my mind. Because a hundred miles didn't work."

"Wyatt." I shook my head and swallowed. Nerves mixed with excitement from his words had my stomach flipping. "I—"

"Boss." Steven's voice interrupted the moment as we continued to stare at each other.

Finally, Wyatt's shoulders dropped, and he turned toward the young guy.

"You're back?"

"Yeah. I decided there was something missing in Boston." He chuckled. "Guess this place is starting to grow on me."

My breath hitched, and although Steven didn't catch it, I didn't miss how Wyatt glanced over at me.

"I'm going to run out and grab some food. Probably pizza from Starlight Pi or maybe Big Chowder this time. What can I bring you two back?"

Before I lost the nerve, or maybe even the chance, I spoke up. "Thought I was going with you?"

Wyatt's gaze spun back to me and his brows rose. "If that's what you want." He tipped his head toward the front door. "You ready? Paul's waiting out front."

Now it was my turn to smirk. Oh. Confident, was he? Odd since I wasn't sure about this insane plan. Or what the hell he was even offering me. He knew I wasn't agreeing to casual sex with my boss, right? And, of course, I couldn't say any of that in front of Steven.

Wyatt turned back to the young guy again. "Mind holding down the fort? I'll bring you your normal back from Big Chowder?"

"Yeah, no problem, and my usual is fine. Thank you."

I walked around the counter, and the minute my feet hit the tiled foyer in front of the desk, I froze. My skin broke out in gooseflesh as Wyatt's heated stare trailed down the black dress I wore and landed on my knee-high black heeled boots. They usually made me feel sexy, but with his hooded stare, that feeling was so much stronger.

"Let's go." The gruffness of his voice made it even better.

I loved the feeling of affecting him like this so much. And as he waved me in front of him toward the front door, I wondered if he knew or understood that.

Once outside, my heels tapped against the concrete as we made our way to the street where Paul was parked. He glanced down at my boots again and his jaw clenched.

"Is this like the thing that happened on Friday? Where my boobs in the sweater I wore were such a distraction you couldn't focus on what I was saying?"

His gaze raised to my face, and he stopped, suddenly turning to me. "Yes. You in come-fuck-me boots is definitely making my good intentions for tonight hard to remember."

I tilted my head. "Good intentions?"

"Yes. Taking you out on a date and keeping my hands to myself."

I smiled. "But what if I don't want you to keep your hands to yourself?"

He quickly crowded my space, his breath dancing along my skin as he leaned forward to whisper in my ear. "And where exactly do you want my hands?"

Heat rose into my face, a stark contrast to the chill air around us. "Anywhere on my bare skin."

He trailed one finger down my arm and a shiver raced through me. I didn't know whether it was the cold March air or his touch or both. Regardless, that simple touch already had me wanting more.

"Come on, you're cold. I have a jacket in the car." He threaded his fingers through mine and pulled me forward.

Once inside, Paul looked over his shoulder at me with a smile. "Nice to see you again."

"You too."

Wyatt held his jacket open for me, and I slipped my arms through the sleeves.

His hand found my knee. "Art on the Square first, Paul."

"Got it." Paul pulled away from the hotel.

"Art on the Square?" I asked.

"Yeah. Local artist. Love her stuff."

I whipped my gaze to him. A light stubble coated his jaw, eliciting thoughts of his face rubbing along my skin, leaving rough sensations behind. I attempted to squeeze my legs together to relieve the tension, forgetting his hand was on my knee until he applied pressure, pulling my right leg back toward him.

He studied me with a smirk, desire swirling in his irises.

"Wyatt?" My voice was barely a whisper.

"Yeah, baby?" he leaned his head back against the seat and turned to look at me.

Those words made me feel even more unsure about all of this, and suddenly I wasn't sure what the hell I was doing. Had I completely lost my mind? But I couldn't say it felt wrong either.

"Angie." He squeezed my knee.

I finally met his gaze and swallowed thickly at the vulnerability there.

"I know I'm asking for a lot of trust that I probably don't even deserve. And I have no idea what I'm doing. But the one thing I know is sitting here with you feels right." He reached up and tucked a piece of hair behind my ear. "Remember, no expectations tonight. Just a date."

I relaxed back into my seat and nodded. "Okay."

A date. I could do that. At least I thought I could.

Paul pulled up in front of a brick storefront where the window showcased several beautiful paintings. I couldn't believe he'd thought to bring me here.

He climbed out and offered me his hand. I scooted over and swung my feet out, loving the way he zeroed in on my legs where the skirt of my dress rose up my thighs. For the first time, I didn't feel the need to yank it back down.

He pulled me to my feet and tight against his chest, burying his nose in my hair and inhaling.

Did he really just smell me? I giggled.

"Honeysuckle," he whispered.

I shivered from his warm breath against my ear. "It's my favorite scent." I had an obsession, and almost all my lotions, perfumes, and bath items had honeysuckle in them.

"It's intoxicating." He pulled back and searched my face as he ran his hand down my arm and threaded his fingers through mine.

We stood there for a heartbeat, staring at each other, before he turned toward the art gallery. I stepped past him as he held the door open, and my jaw dropped. Gorgeous paintings of the lighthouse, the beach, and the town hung around the small space. One in particular caught my eye, and I moved toward it.

"It's the hotel," I said in awe. The wraparound porch with the lights, the red door that seemed to pop from the page against the hues of white and lighter browns, the large windows that displayed bouquets of flowers—it was all there, in brilliant, realistic brushstrokes.

He came to stand next to me. "Stella did such a great job on this one."

I whipped my gaze his way. "How come you haven't bought it? I'm surprised your grandmother didn't want it."

"I do own it." He didn't look away from the piece as he talked. "She was still finishing it when Nana B passed. I bought it once she was done, but I wanted it displayed here so everyone in town could see it whenever they wanted. I wasn't the only one grieving, and it felt selfish to keep it for myself."

I smiled. "You're such a romantic."

Finally, his gaze left the painting to land on me with an eyebrow raised. "No one has ever used that word to describe me."

I rolled my eyes. "Must be getting soft in your old age, then. Because that is the most sentimental thing I've ever heard."

A woman appeared in the room, and the moment Wyatt turned toward her, she closed the distance, holding her arms out.

"Wyatt, so glad you could come."

I wished I could say I wasn't jealous when they embraced, but I'd be lying. She was gorgeous, with long strawberry blond hair and a figure I'd die for.

"Is this Angie?" She turned to look at me as she pulled back.

Who was this woman? And how did she know my name?

"It is." He peered down at me, and his hand landed on the small of my back. "Angie, this is Stella."

"You painted all these?" Her work was utterly beautiful.

She nodded with a smile.

"Angie loves your painting of the doors from New Orleans."

"Wait." I glanced from Wyatt to Stella. "That was you too?"

She nodded. "Yeah. I grew up there." She pointed behind her to a painting of a large, beautiful riverboat. "That one is my favorite."

"It's gorgeous. But the one with all the doors is captivating. I love the way they seem to pop off the page." I turned back to the painting of the front of the hotel. "Like the red door does in this one."

Wyatt led me to the opposite wall. "This one is my favorite. The way the waves come alive."

They did. Looking around, most of her paintings had that feel. Slightly subdued backgrounds with either bright pops of color or a technique that made it almost look 3D.

We spent another few minutes chatting with her before she stepped away to chat with a man who walked in. Wyatt led me into a large, open room that had a dozen more paintings. I was in awe and enjoyed looking at her work as we walked around and stopped at each one. Was it sad that, so far, this was the best date I'd ever been on? The fact that Wyatt put thought into what I'd enjoy?

I turned toward him and popped up on my toes, pressing my lips to his cheek. "Thank you for this."

"For what?" He cocked a brow. "You haven't even decided which one I'm buying you yet."

Was he out of his mind? "Buy me one? You can't buy me a thousand-dollar painting."

"Why not?" His brows pulled together. "It's not like I don't have the money, and it's something you like."

I opened my mouth and then closed it again with a sigh. "No expectations, remember? And you buying me stuff on our first date feels like a lot of expectations. So how about for tonight, we table the idea of buying expensive art?"

His face fell and his lips turned down into the cutest pout. "Told you I'm not good at this."

I spun so I was standing directly in front of him. Using both hands to grab the sides of his dress shirt where it was open at the top, I pulled him down toward me and pressed my lips against his. He stiffened for a breath before relaxing and grasping my waist, yanking me tightly against his body. Before I could even take another breath, he was devouring my mouth like he was dying of thirst and I was the drink of water he needed to survive.

It was a heady feeling when his cock hardened and pushed against my lower belly. A groan vibrated through him, and he broke the kiss.

"Jesus, woman. How do you do that?"

"Do what?"

"Make me lose all sense of control and intelligent thought." He sighed and rested his forehead against mine. "I have no idea what we were talking about."

I chuckled and pulled back to look up at him. "You wanted to buy me a painting, and I reminded you of the no-expectations thing. But then you said you weren't good at this."

"Right." The pout was back on his face. "So why'd you kiss me?"

"Because bringing me here, to walk around and look at beautiful paintings, was perfect. I don't need you to buy me one." I reached up and ran my finger along his lower lip, wiping off the red lipstick smeared there. "And I wanted to show you how perfect this is."

"Most women want me to buy them things."

I raised a brow. "And do you think I'm like those women?"

He studied me for a beat before his head shook slightly. "I think you're unlike anyone I've ever met."

"I hope that's a good thing," I said wearily.

"It's uncharted territory for me." His grip tightened on my waist as he continued to hold me flush against him. Almost as if he was worried I was about to disappear. "I've never been this freaked out about messing up. I'm not afraid to own my shit. But with you..."

Uncertainty flashed across his features, and I ran my hands up his chest and around to the back of his neck. "The no expectations rule applies for you too. I don't expect you to be perfect or not mess up. All I expect is honesty."

"That I can do." A smile lit his face. "Ready for dinner?"

I nodded, and excitement bubbled up at the reminder that the night wasn't over yet.

Chapter Fifteen

WYATT

SITTING across from Angie in my favorite restaurant had me more excited than anything I'd experienced with any other woman. Her love for food was perfection. She popped a piece of fried clam in her mouth and closed her eyes, savoring the taste, and I was so glad I suggested trying them as an appetizer.

Would she look entranced like that when she took my cock into her mouth?

Fuck. I needed to think about something else. If not, there was no way I was getting up from my seat without it being obvious exactly what I was thinking about.

"What do you do in Boston?" she asked as she reached for another piece of fried clam.

"What do you mean?"

"Like, for work."

I sat back in my chair and crossed my arms over my chest. I wasn't quite sure how to answer her question. Would she judge me? But I promised honesty.

"I don't work."

Her brows shot to her hairline. "What do you mean?"

"I don't need to work." I smirked at the confusion marring her face. "My parents left me enough money that I would likely never need an actual job. I invest a lot of it. I'm on the board of two different charities, and I manage all aspects of the business side of the hotel now. But I don't work."

I didn't see judgment on her face, but shock was definitely there. She blinked a few times before finally shaking her head. "I don't think I could do that. Doesn't it get boring?"

I shrugged. "Sometimes. But I try to fill my time with things I enjoy or that I'm good at."

"I guess it would be nice to have the freedom to do that."

She moaned around the food in her mouth, and I smirked.

"I could watch you eat all night, you know."

She froze and raised a brow. "Watch me eat?"

"Yeah. It's sexy as hell."

"I highly doubt that."

Sometimes I forgot how unaware she was of her own sex appeal. I made sure I was safe to stand before getting up and moving to sit next to her in the booth. We were in the back corner against the far wall of the restaurant, so, luckily, we had plenty of privacy.

I grabbed her hand and placed it on my crotch. "All from watching you eat."

Her adorable giggle had my dick jumping against her hand, and her breath hitched again. I expected her to yank her hand away, but instead, she cupped me through my pants, and I fucking almost lost it.

"Don't tease me." I leaned close to her ear and held her hand tight in mine.

She smirked, looking up at me. "And what if I don't listen?"

I let go of her hand, leaving it in my lap, and moved mine to her bare leg. Trailing it up under her dress, I paused halfway up her thigh. "Two can play that game if that's what you want."

"You make me feel sexy, Wyatt." Her voice was barely a whisper. "It's not something I'm used to."

"Well, you should be." Painfully slowly, I inched my hand farther up. "Any man who hasn't made you feel like a queen he's worshipping isn't doing it right." Dying to touch her, I couldn't stop my hand from drifting up her smooth skin, my pinky brushing along her panties. "The first time we're together, you're going to sit on my face, and I'm going to show you exactly how a man should make you feel."

She gasped, and her teeth pressed into her bottom lip as I trailed my pinky finger along the outside of the lace material. The waiter approached the table, and she shifted under my touch. I gripped her thigh, preventing her from moving away from me as the server asked if we were ready to order.

I nodded. "I'll take the veal parmigiana." I moved my finger back and forth along the same path from a moment ago, eliciting a slight shiver from her, and glanced at her with a smirk. "What did you decide you wanted?"

Her cheeks held a hint of pink as I continued teasing her with the tip of my finger, and heat radiated off her in waves. Her gaze was locked on the menu in front of her, and her chest rose and fell as she attempted to control her breathing.

I paused and moved my finger away, giving her a moment to focus and order her food. As she pulled herself together and ordered, stumbling through the process, I held back the laugh that bubbled up.

"I hate you," she mumbled once the waiter stepped away again.

"I think you liked that." I leaned closer to her and lowered my voice another octave. "I'd bet your panties are soaking wet right now."

"Don't get too cocky there." She smirked at me. "I don't sleep with guys on the first date."

"I distinctly remember you saying you would have let me fuck you on Saturday if I hadn't stopped it."

She shrugged. "Maybe. But now you might have to work for it." She pulled her lip between her teeth as she fought a smile.

Her words were teasing, but I wanted her to know I wasn't taking it lightly either. "I'm okay with that. I plan on showing you I'm serious. And as much as I'm dying to taste you, to feel you grip my cock and scream out my name, I want to take it slow. To make sure you know that's not all I want."

She searched my face, and I struggled to tell if she believed my words or not. I removed my hand from under her dress and positioned my arm around her shoulders instead.

She sighed and melted into my side, laying her head on my shoulder. "What about Boston?" Her words held a hint of trepidation.

"What about it?"

"You said that's been your home?" She paused before adding, "Would you live here full time or split your time between here and there?"

I swallowed but reminded myself that she wanted honesty. "I would have to travel to Boston for meetings here and there. But here with you would be my home."

She was so quiet I was nervous I'd said the wrong thing.

"I like the sound of that."

I smiled, pulling her closer and pressing a kiss to the top of her head. "Me too."

This felt so right, and I was kicking myself for not realizing it when I kissed her Saturday night. But she was here now, in my arms, and I wanted to make every moment with her count.

Be all the things I thought she deserved but never thought I could be.

Chapter Sixteen

ANGIE

I STEPPED BACK and surveyed the staff lounge that was set up for the catered lunch. Not that I could really appreciate my efforts, because my mind was elsewhere. Specifically, stuck on Wyatt Reed and how amazing last night had been. Getting involved with my boss had never been on my bingo card. Except now it was, and I should be freaking out, but I wasn't.

Instead, I had our date on repeat in my head. Thinking about how when we got back to the suite, he kissed me until we were both breathless. And then pressed his lips tenderly against my forehead, sending me off to bed with promises that he intended to show me all the things I deserved.

. . .

My phone vibrated in my back pocket, and I pulled it out.

Izzy: Why didn't you tell me you were dating Wyatt Reed?
    Me: What? How do you even know that??

Although we didn't have that exact conversation, I didn't have any doubts that was exactly what we were doing.

Izzy: Because he's hot and famous and you guys are 🔥🔥🔥 but just don't read the comments. The trolls are just jealous.
    Me: What. Are. You. Talking about?
    Izzy: The picture of you two at dinner.
    Izzy: Crap. I forgot you don't do social media.
    Izzy: Here... *Picture of Wyatt sitting next to me whispering in my ear*

What the picture didn't show was his hand between my legs.

Izzy: You guys are adorable. How'd you meet and why didn't you tell me?
    Me: He's my boss

I sighed when her name flashed across my screen, swiping to answer and bringing the phone to my ear.

"What the hell, Angie? Wyatt Reed is your boss? The owner of that hotel?"

"Yes. Now explain why someone took a picture of us and why you think he's famous."

I mean yeah, he was rich, but as far as my Google search went, he didn't seem famous for anything.

"He dated that blond actress you like. What was her name... Kelly? Kylie? Kennedy? Anyway, after that, he became super popular on social media. And when they broke up, he became Instagram famous as Boston's most eligible bachelor."

My head whipped up as Wyatt stepped into the doorway, his gaze immediately seeking me out.

"Izzy, gotta go. Call you later."

I hung up and stared at Wyatt.

"What's wrong?" He closed the distance, and I continued to stare up at him.

"Nothing." My voice squeaked, and I cleared my throat, refusing to glance down at my phone. But I lost that battle.

His gaze followed mine, landing on the picture of us.

"Oh." He looked up with raised brows. "Please tell me you didn't read the comments."

"No." I narrowed my eyes. "But since you're the second person who's said that, I think I should."

He shook his head. "I wouldn't. Some people have nothing better to do than dump on other people's lives."

"They're all probably wondering why you're out to dinner with someone like me when you could be dating a model or actress or something."

He stepped forward and grabbed my waist, pulling me toward him. "I don't care what they think. I don't want anyone but you. But a lot of the comments are attacking the playboy lifestyle they're used to seeing. Just so you're prepared."

I sagged against him, letting him wrap his arms around me and bring me flush against him.

"This looks great."

"Huh?"

"The lunch spread." He examined the room. "It looks good, and the flowers are a nice touch."

"Oh." I stepped back, pride rising in my chest as I surveyed the space. It really had come together nicely. "I didn't really have anything to go off. Hope it's close to what your grand-mother has done in years past."

He wrapped his arm around my shoulders and pressed his lips to my temple. "I think she'd be proud, and everyone will love it."

My stomach flipped. No one would believe Wyatt Reed was capable of this type of tenderness.

"Dinner tonight? Like in the suite. I want to cook for you."

I peered up at him. "You cook?"

He shrugged. "My grandmother taught me how to make a few simple things. Nothing that special." His hand ran up and down my arm, the simple touch doing crazy things to my body. "Unless you want to go out to dinner again."

I assumed going out again meant more prying eyes. Was he trying to avoid that?

"If we go out again, more pictures of us could be posted on social media."

"I don't care what pictures they take or post of us. But I understand if it bothers you. You should know, though..." He trailed off before looking down at me with caution. "It has become more of a constant thing in my life over the years. But most of the time, I ignore it. It's not usually a big deal here, but it is when I'm in Boston."

Voices close by had me stepping away from him and straightening my sweater. I held back the eye roll as his lips turned down into a frown. Was he intending to make it obvious in front of all the staff today? We'd eventually need to deal with that, but I didn't think right now was the time.

I busied myself with talking to the employees and thanking them. During a lull in the action, I looked around and noticed Wyatt was gone.

My phone vibrated on one of the tables where I'd set it down, and I picked it up. Wyatt's name in the notifications sent excitement coursing through me as I opened our text thread.

WYATT: Dinner? 7p.m.?

MY FINGERS FLEW across the screen without a second thought.

ME: Definitely. Looking forward to tasting your masterpiece.

Wyatt: Don't get too excited. But are you sure? I don't mind going out again if you'd prefer.

UPSTAIRS ALONE IN the suite with him? That idea alone was causing my core to throb with anticipation. I wanted this. Him. More than I'd ever wanted anything. And that made the answer to his question easy.

ME: I'm more than sure.

Chapter Seventeen

WYATT

JESUS CHRIST. What was she trying to do to me? The black dress she wore hugged the top part of her body, including right above her hips, before flaring out around her thighs. It also barely covered much—not typical of the dresses she usually wore that ended above her knees. I was one hundred percent positive if she bent over, I'd get a glimpse of her luscious ass. Hopefully clad in only a thong.

I didn't even try to hide the fact that I was drinking her in as I let my gaze trail down her body, ending at her sky-high heels. I needed to remember to tell her to leave those on when I drilled into her.

Wait. I blinked. No. That wasn't what we were doing tonight. Just dinner, I reminded myself again. Showing her what she deserved.

A seductive chuckle left her lips, causing me to raise my eyes back to her face. I cocked a brow. Could she read my mind? Was my need for her written all over my face? I wouldn't be surprised if that was the case.

"I'm starting to love when you zone out now."

"Huh?"

"I asked you what you were making. But I'm pretty sure you didn't hear me because you were drooling over my legs."

I shrugged. "I love your legs." Especially if they were wrapped around my waist, or my head. I shook my head, trying to concentrate on the conversation. "I'm making baked chicken and potatoes. It's super easy and basic."

"Smells amazing."

I turned back to my task of plating everything. "Our wine is already on the balcony with the small gas fire pit going." With a glance over my shoulder, I added, "But it's chillier out there than it was last week. So we can eat inside if you want."

She shook her head. "I'd like to try outside. I'll grab a throw to cover my legs."

I hated that idea, but I didn't want her to be cold either, so I nodded. The black dress she wore had long sleeves, but when she turned, I almost tripped as I moved behind her, plates in hand. The fabric dropped into a V down her back.

Jesus. Maybe this was a test to see how quickly I'd come undone. As if on cue, my dick sprang to life.

I set our plates down and took my seat across from her. The way her hair shimmered in the glow of the fire held me captive. I reluctantly pulled my gaze away and focused on the plate in front of me.

The first few minutes were silent. The crashing of the waves echoed around us, but it wasn't an awkward silence. It was filled with tension and longing. And I didn't believe that was only on my end, because every time I snuck a glance at her, she was looking at me too. In those glimpses, I saw so much desire in her eyes it was torture.

The way, and with such intensity, I wanted her was utterly new to me. I didn't only want sex. I wanted to spend hours exploring her body. Hours making her feel good. All goddamn night inside her if she'd let me. And then hold her in my arms until morning. That was something I'd never even considered before now.

"This is good."

I looked up, blinking at her. "Huh?"

Shit. I'd zoned out again. I tried to hide the smirk, but I failed.

She shook her head. "The food. It's really good." She popped a piece of potato in her mouth and moaned around the fork.

I stared at her, totally tuned in to her every move as she brought the fork out of her mouth slowly, running her tongue along the underside. Images of her taking my cock into her pretty little mouth in exactly the same way flashed through my mind. I shifted, fighting off a groan.

She pulled her bottom lip into her mouth as she forked another piece and then repeated the same motions.

"You like teasing me?" I raised a brow.

"I like the way you make me feel when you look at me like that." She brought the fork back to her mouth and took a bite.

I mimicked the action, taking another bite of my own food. "How do I look at you?" Could she see the intense desire that I constantly felt around her?

"Like you want to rip my clothes off and have your way with me."

I nodded. "It's so much more than that, Angie. And it's a

first for me." I held her gaze, hoping she could see the truth behind my words. "I'm dying to taste you—"

Her breath hitched and her pupils dilated. But I wasn't done.

"To touch you, explore every inch of your body, then make you come on my cock over and over again until we're both spent."

Her eyes darkened to an almost black and her gorgeous tits heaved up and down as her breathing sped up.

"But then I want to fall asleep with you in my arms." I reached across the table and laid my hand on top of hers. "And I'll spend however long it'll take showing you exactly that."

After another minute of silence, she spoke in a barely there whisper. "I want that too. All of that."

Part of me came alive with excitement at what her words meant, but then I quickly squashed that excitement. I wanted —no, needed—her to be sure. Because the minute I had her, she would be mine.

I swallowed and took a breath, putting together my thoughts before opening my mouth. It wasn't something that came easy, but I had to be better, and she made me want to do that.

"Angie," I reached across the table again and took her hand. "I want you to be sure." I shook my head when she opened her mouth to respond and went on, "Tonight I want to eat dinner with you and then sit together by the fire. We don't have to rush the other stuff."

She let out a sigh and smiled at me. "When you say the most perfect things like that, it makes me want you more."

I brought my fork to my mouth again. "I'm not trying to say perfect things, only honest things."

She shook her head and began eating again. "Tell me how you became Instagram famous."

I groaned. Jesus, I should have seen this coming, but the last thing I wanted to do was talk about one of my exes.

"My sister said you dated one of my favorite actresses, so I gotta know."

I nodded. "Kennedy was great, and our relationship was okay. But she was filming a TV show when we started dating, and I was in my sophomore year of college. So we barely saw each other. And I don't think either of us was invested enough to make it work."

"Why do I feel like there's something you're not telling me?"

Fuck. I'd be lying if I said her being able to read me so well didn't freak me out a bit. I pushed my plate away and sat back in my chair.

"Honesty, remember?" She stared at me expectantly.

"After things ended with Kennedy, I met someone else." I crossed my arms. "It ended very badly, and after that, I decided I wasn't cut out for serious relationships."

Her brows rose slightly. Exactly what I was trying to avoid. I needed her to know I was done carrying that baggage around. Angie wasn't Amanda.

"Until now," I added.

"Now... you think you are?"

"I'm willing to try." I shrugged. "I don't know. With you it feels... easier, I guess, or maybe more intense. But more importantly, you are the first woman in almost eight years who makes me want something more. So, I think that speaks volumes."

She smiled and set her fork down before grabbing her glass of wine. I stood, holding my own glass, and offered her my hand, ready to be closer to her. Her fingers laced through mine, and I led her around the table to the double chaise lounge that sat next to the fire pit. It was plenty big enough for both of us, but I obviously would allow her to take the other one if she wanted space.

After putting our glasses on the small table, I positioned myself on one side and patted the seat next to me. "Join me?"

She eyed the space next to me with a raised brow, but after a moment of indecision, she lay down next to me. I stretched out my arm and she curled into the crook of it.

Damn, it all felt so perfect.

We lay like that, sipping our wines, until I felt her shiver.

"Are you cold? I can grab the blanket you brought out. Or we can go inside if you want."

She shook her head and looked up at me. "Not cold."

Desire swam in her eyes and she leaned up, pressing her lips to mine, catching me off guard. She pulled back, searching my face. For what, I didn't know, but I could clearly see want and vulnerability there.

I wouldn't stop this, but maybe I could give us both something we wanted without rushing into sex. Threading my fingers through her short locks, I brought her mouth back to mine and devoured her. Nothing was slow about the kiss as our mouths fused and our tongues dueled.

Gripping her knee and pulling it across my leg so her core laid flush against my thigh, I moved her slightly against me and swallowed down the moan that slipped up her throat. I wanted to make her feel good, but I'd been dying to taste her, so I broke the kiss and slid down the lounge until I was almost flat.

"Straddle me, baby."

Her brows rose high on her forehead. "What?"

"Do you trust me?"

She pulled her bottom lip into her mouth and nodded. "Yeah."

"Good." I tugged her leg, and she came willingly to straddle my stomach. "I want you to come on my tongue."

Her eyes widened. "I—"

"Please, baby. I've been dying to find out how you taste,

and I want to watch those tits bounce above me as you ride my face."

Her pupils blew out and her teeth pressed into her bottom lip again.

"You want that, don't you?"

Her cheeks flushed as she nodded.

"Get that pussy up here, then." I slid farther down the chaise and slipped my arms one by one between her legs.

She froze, inches away from where she needed to be, a mix of desire and uncertainty in her gaze as she stared down at me. "I don't... I mean I've never..." She blew out a harsh breath.

Fuck. Would I be the first to give her this experience? That spurred me on even more. "You trust me, remember?"

She nodded.

I ran my finger along the crease of her ass, following her thong, and she bucked against my hand as I brushed my fingers over her warm and soaking-wet panties. "Lift your dress up. Let me see how wet you are for me."

Her gaze swiveled from right to left, quickly looking around the large balcony area.

"Don't worry, no one can see us. We're on the corner, remember?"

Her head bobbed again, and she lifted her dress, bunching it around her waist. I pulled the fabric of her thong to the side, and my gaze locked on her glistening pussy. My dick pushed against the fabric of my pants as I took her in.

"Now I want you to ride my face and don't stop until you're coming on my tongue." I gripped her ass and pulled her to me until she was exactly where I wanted her.

Her free hand shot out and she braced against the raised head of the lounge chair. Her tits strained against the neckline of her dress, threatening to pop out at any second. The view I had was fucking amazing. I wanted to savor it for as long as I could.

"Oh my god." She bucked hard against my hold as I moved her roughly back and forth along my tongue. I set the rhythm for her, showing her how to grind herself against my mouth. It didn't take long for her to take over.

"Wyatt," she moaned, staring down at me as she rotated her pussy in circles against my tongue. "This feels so good."

Her movements picked up and she threw her head back, her full tits bouncing above me, and I couldn't wait to do this again. But next time she wouldn't be wearing any clothes. I tapped her ass lightly, making her look back down at me. I wanted to watch her as she came.

I moved her slightly, plunging my tongue into her and reaching up to grab each mound of her breasts. A deep moan vibrated through her and her movements became more erratic. She continued to grind against my face as I thrust into her over and over.

"Oh, fuck," she said breathlessly. "Right there. Don't stop."

I had no plans to stop. I would do this all night long if I needed to. Watching her was my pleasure.

Her body shook as her wetness coated my mouth. She rode out her orgasm, little moans of ecstasy escaping her, and her gaze stayed locked on me. It was by far the most intimate experience I'd ever had.

And I wanted more. More of this. More of her.

Chapter Eighteen

ANGIE

I SAGGED BACK, utterly spent from the orgasm that had rolled through me like a freight train. I glanced back down, taking in the pride on this crazy man's face. Pride. At getting me off. I loved it. I'd never had a man ever care about my pleasure or whether I came or not. In fact, going down on me was not really a common occurrence, let alone letting me come on their face.

I wanted to make him feel as good as he had made me feel. Letting my dress fall back into place, I shimmied down his body. It was obvious what he was trying to do tonight, and I respected it. But it didn't mean he couldn't be pleased too.

He watched me as I continued my way down until I was straddling his legs, but his hands caught mine as I went for the button of his pants. "No, baby. Tonight was about you."

I shook my head. "You got to taste me, now I want to taste you."

His eyes darkened, but he quickly shook his head. "I want nothing more than to see that pretty red mouth wrapped around my cock—"

"Good. Then let me." I ran a hand along the outline of his cock through his pants.

He groaned, throwing his head back against the cushion of the seat, his jaw locked tight. This time, when I went for the button of his pants again, he let me undo it and unzip them. I pulled out his long, thick cock and licked my lips as I fisted it in my hand, watching as precum coated the tip.

"Fuck, baby." He looked back down at me as I moved my hand up and down. "Take me in your mouth."

I smirked up at him. "Please?"

His fingers threaded through my hair, and he tugged. "Please put your lips around me so I can fuck that sassy little mouth of yours."

God, I never realized I would get so turned on by dirty talk. I leaned down and covered his tip with my mouth before sliding down until he reached the back of my throat.

"Jesus." He pulled on my hair, forcing me back up. "Do that again."

His words spurred me on as I slid back down. He bucked up and I swallowed, making more room in the back of my throat before raising back up. I moved up and down, allowing him to use the grip on my hair to help set the pace he wanted.

"You going to take it in your mouth like a good girl?"

I nodded, wanting nothing more than to give him this. To taste him on my tongue.

"Fuck," he ground out. "I'm gonna come, baby."

His cock pulsed and he filled my mouth as he held my gaze. The saltiness coated my tongue before I sucked and swallowed, pulling every last drop from him.

"You coming on my face was by far the sexiest thing I've ever seen. But watching you take my cock is a close second."

He brushed the hair back from my face, the tenderness making me want so much more. I smiled and tucked him back into his pants.

"Come here." He held his arm out and patted his chest.

I climbed off his legs and positioned myself in the crook of his arm, laying my head back on his chest. I sagged into him, letting my eyes drift closed until I shivered, finally feeling the chilly air against my skin.

He shifted out from beneath me, and I opened my eyes as he stood, offering me his hand. I took it and let him lead me into his bedroom through the other door. I swallowed, not exactly sure where this was going.

He pulled a drawer open and turned to me, holding out what looked like a T-shirt and a pair of boxers. "I want to sleep in the same bed tonight. No sex. At least not tonight," he added with a smirk. "Just hold you and sleep."

Butterflies took off in my stomach. How was I already falling for this man?

"Unless you don't want that—"

"No," I blurted. "I do." I turned around. "Can you help me with the zipper?"

His fingers brushed along my back as he unzipped my dress. I turned back toward him and took the clothes he offered before scurrying past him into the master bath. I had come on his face, and he'd seen me half naked, but I wasn't ready to fully undress in front of him yet.

I still didn't quite understand why he wanted me when he could have a model or actress or whatever, but I tried not to question it.

I returned to find him already in bed. He held the covers up and I climbed in, reclaiming my position on his chest.

"Okay. Third sexiest thing I've ever seen... you in my clothes."

I smiled and let my eyes drift closed, praying that this was real.

Chapter Nineteen

WYATT

I PULLED out my phone and brought up the text thread with Angie. I'd planned on giving her the day off to send her to the spa, but that was back when I didn't realize how much I'd miss having her around.

I hesitated, my fingers hovering over the keypad on my phone. She was supposed to be relaxing, taking the day off. The last thing she needed was me smothering her. Before I could decide about sending her another text, three dots appeared. I couldn't stop the smile that broke out on my face as I waited for her text to come through.

"People are going to start thinking something's wrong if you keep this up."

I glanced up at Paul, who stood in the doorway of my office, shaking his head.

"Keep what up?"

"Smiling all the time and sending staff home early."

I shrugged. "He was sick."

Paul chuckled. "More like hungover."

Was he serious? "Why do you think that?"

My phone chimed and I looked back down.

ANGIE: Yes, I really enjoyed the spa. Thank you so much for arranging it.

THREE DOTS APPEARED and disappeared in rapid succession before her next text came through.

ANGIE: Do you have plans for dinner? Was thinking I could pick up a few pizzas at Starlight Pi.

I SMILED and typed out a reply.

ME: No plans for dinner. Only for dessert.
     Angie: Oh?
     Me: Yeah, last night, I found my new favorite treat.
     Angie: blushing emoji.

. . .

A THROAT CLEARING pulled my attention, and I looked back up at Paul.

He tipped his chin toward the phone in my hand. "I'm assuming that's Angie that has you hyper focused on your phone at the moment."

I nodded. He didn't need a response. His smirk said it all.

"I'm pretty sure I've never seen you lovesick like this."

"I'm not..." I started to shake my head but stopped. I didn't need to finish that statement. We both knew any type of denial would be a lie. I could tell him she was more like an obsession. That I couldn't possibly be in love with someone after a week. But that would be a lie too.

He chuckled. "I'll let you know when she's ready to be picked up." He raised a brow at me before adding, "Assuming you want to ride with me?"

"Think she'd be annoyed?"

"Nope." He shook his head. "That girl has it just as bad."

I shot up, my back snapping straight. Paul laughed as he turned and walked away.

Was he just saying that? Or did she feel as strongly about me as I did her? I typed out another text.

ME: So, pizza for dinner and you for dessert?

I LEANED BACK and closed my eyes, picturing her above me as she let herself go. I wanted so damn badly to see that same expression on her face as I plowed into her for the first time.

Another chime indicated she'd responded, and I smiled as I read her text.

. . .

ANGIE: Only if I get to have dessert too.

MY DICK SPRANG to life as the memory of her with my cock in her mouth flashed through my mind.

Chapter Twenty

ANGIE

I STEPPED up to the counter and gave the older lady my order. I figured ordering the same three kinds of pizza Wyatt had ordered that first night we ate together would be safe.

The woman behind the counter smiled at me as she tilted her head. "I think Blanche was right."

"What?" My brow pulled together at the odd response.

"She was convinced she'd found the perfect woman for Wyatt." The lady chuckled. "And between the picture of you two at dinner, talk of Wyatt bouncing around the hotel like he's on cloud nine, and then him calling a little bit ago asking me to put whatever you order on his tab, I would say I have to agree."

I shook my head but couldn't stop the smile. How much pizza did he think I was planning to order?

"He also said you'd love our bruschetta and oversized cookies."

I glanced at the display case that housed the desserts. The large chocolate chunk cookies did look amazing, but so did the chocolate fudge walnut ones.

Was Wyatt intent on making my thighs even larger than they were? I sighed. "Okay. Add the bruschetta and..." I studied the cookie selection again. "One of the chocolate chunk cookies, please."

The lady's brows furrowed like I'd confused her, but she nodded and stepped away. Five minutes later, my phone chimed, and I glanced down at it, swiping open the text from Wyatt.

WYATT: Fuck, you're so beautiful it hurts.

I STARED at it for a minute before sensing someone step up behind me and spinning around to see him standing there, close enough I had to tilt my head back to look up at him.

"What are you—"

Before I could finish my question, he reached out and latched a strong, warm hand to my hip, pulling me closer.

He leaned down, his breath skating along my ear. "I missed you."

A shiver shot through me, and I leaned back, our lips inches apart. He searched my face before erasing the space, his lips brushing gently against mine. I could tell he was holding back as his fingers tightened on my waist and his lips continued to move against mine.

A throat clearing had him pulling back with a smirk. In my lust induced haze, it didn't register who'd cleared their throat or why until Wyatt stepped around me to grab the food.

"Thank you." Wyatt shot her a wink. "One of each?"

She nodded. "Of course."

"You're the best." He turned with way too much food in his hands, and I fell in step beside him as we headed for the door.

My curiosity got the best of me before we reached the door. "What did you mean by one of each?"

"Their cookies. I asked her to give us one of each."

"Wyatt." His name came out in a huff.

He pushed the door open with his back, holding it open as he raised a brow. "What? Do you not like cookies or something?"

"Of course I like cookies." Now I sounded exasperated. How was that even a legitimate question? "It's obvious by the size of my thighs that I like cookies."

His expression turned hard. "Good. I fucking love your thighs. So if eating cookies will guarantee they keep my head locked between your legs, I'll make sure to feed you cookies every day."

I rolled my eyes. "It might guarantee I suffocate you next time."

He chuckled darkly. "That isn't the threat you think it is."

"God, you're impossible."

He stopped a few feet before we reached the car, and I turned to look at him.

"How about a compromise?"

I raised a skeptical brow. From the playfulness in his voice, I had a feeling he didn't really have a true compromise.

"We'll eat pizza and cookies until you're utterly satisfied, then you can ride my face again until you're breathless and spent."

Heat skirted up my neck into my face as my core throbbed from his words. I wanted to do that again, but I also wanted so much more. I wanted to feel him inside of me so much I'd spent almost all day thinking of what it would be like.

"Can I ride your cock too? That might be even more of a workout."

His eyes widened for a heartbeat before they turned almost completely dark. He was speechless, and I took the moment to fuel my confidence as I stepped closer to him, crowding his space this time.

"I think that's a better compromise, don't you think?" I batted my eyelashes and placed my hand on his biceps, feeling the muscles twitch under my touch.

I loved that I could affect him like he did me.

Turning away from him, I walked to the car and climbed into the backseat. Once he was seated next to me and Paul had pulled away from the curb, Wyatt's free hand found my thigh, positioning so close to the top his pinky was almost touching the spot that needed his touch the most.

He leaned over and brought his mouth close to my ear. Every time he did that, his warm breath sent the best sensations shooting through my body.

"Angie, I need you to be sure." He pulled back just enough so he could look into my eyes. "I want us both to know without a doubt that you're mine." His lips lifted into that cocky, sexy smile of his.

I studied his face and searched for the right words. Words that would make him believe I trusted him. Trusted us, and this crazy thing between us. I didn't want to wait any longer to be with him.

And while I couldn't find the right words, I hoped my

actions spoke loud enough as I leaned forward and brought my lips to his. His free arm left my thigh and wrapped around my shoulders, bringing me closer as he devoured my mouth.

Breathless and turned on, I didn't even care about food by the time we pulled up to the hotel. It was obvious the only thing I wanted was him.

Chapter Twenty-One

WYATT

As we made our way through the lobby, I prayed no one stopped us. I wanted to feed my girl and then spend all night inside her.

"Wyatt?" my restaurant manager's voice rang out from behind me.

Fuck. I knew it. It wouldn't be that easy. I spun toward her, and by the look on her face, it was obvious this was going to be an issue that required me for more than a few minutes.

I passed the food off to Angie, praying she could read my expression. "Why don't you go ahead up and get yourself some food. Hopefully I won't be long."

Her lips turned down into the cutest pout. I was happy to know she was feeling the same way.

"Go ahead." I tipped my head toward the elevators. "I'll be right behind you."

She nodded with a sigh, and once the elevator door closed behind her, I followed Jenny into the restaurant to deal with whatever issue she needed my help with.

Thankfully the issue wasn't anything time consuming. She needed my approval for an expedited order on a new refrigerator. The restaurant had two in the kitchen, and one of them had failed right before the dinner rush. I'd give my approval for ten refrigerators if it meant it got me upstairs to Angie faster.

I entered the suite and was surprised that Angie was nowhere to be seen. Had she changed her mind? Or was she waiting for me to eat? The food sat on the kitchen island, untouched from what I could tell.

Walking around the front of the island, I found her boots —one, and then a foot away, almost in a line, the other one. Then my gaze locked on her sweater laying another foot down the hallway that led to my bedroom. In fact, I could now make out a line of clothes.

I adjusted myself, my cock now pushing uncomfortably against my pants. I tracked the breadcrumbs of fabric until I got to the last piece, bending to scoop up her silky black panties. Stepping through the doorway, I locked eyes with her. She was curled up under the blankets. Naked. In my bed. Waiting for me.

I fought the ironic laugh that threatened to bubble up. I'd always taken these moments so casually, and now I was nervous as fuck. Ironic wasn't a strong enough word to explain it.

I held her stare as I brought the black fabric up to my nose, breathing in her intoxicating scent. "Did you decide you wanted to work up a sweat first and then eat?"

A smirk lifted her lips. "I decided I couldn't wait any longer to feel you inside me."

My whole body came alive at her words, and I hastily removed my tie, undoing the buttons of my shirt before discarding that just as rapidly.

I moved quickly to the side of the bed and tipped my chin toward her. "Take the covers off." I had no intention of letting her hide her gorgeous body from me. I would spend forever worshipping it if that was what she needed to see how sexy and beautiful she was.

She fiddled with the hem of the blankets, and I unbuttoned my pants, waiting for her to show me the body I'd been fantasizing about.

"Baby, let me see you." I tugged slightly on the edge. "I love your body. Let me show you how fucking gorgeous you are."

She smiled hesitantly but slowly peeled the covers back. Almost immediately, she crossed her arms over her stomach.

"Come here." I beckoned her toward me with my finger.

"Wyatt." She looked down at the sheets. "I'm not—I mean... I know I'm not like the women you usually do this with."

"Damn right."

Her gaze popped up and her eyes widened.

"You are so different from anyone I've ever been with. In almost every way imaginable. The way you make me feel, how sexy you are, even that you're not afraid to tell me when I'm being an ass. All of it makes you different and makes this a first for me."

A flush tinted her cheeks, and she opened her mouth to respond, but I went on.

"Want to know the biggest difference? I want so much more than sex with you. I want to spend all night memorizing every inch of your body. I can't say the same for any of the women I've dated in the last eight years. So please, come here so I can show you exactly how different you are."

Her smile held almost none of the hesitancy it had moments earlier as she got up on her knees.

"You know you're different too."

She crawled across the bed toward me, and I guided her back to her knees in front of me so I could look at her. Memorize all her gorgeous curves.

"How so?" I stepped back, taking in every detail. This time she didn't try to hide from me.

"Most of the guys I've been with don't care if I hide under the blankets or turn off the lights."

Quickly, I discarded the rest of my clothing. "They're all a bunch of idiots, then."

I cupped a full breast in each hand, loving that her nipples pebbled immediately against my thumbs.

She threw her head back with a moan as I continued to tease and play with her perfect tits. I couldn't imagine not getting to play with these. Not getting to watch them bounce as she rode my cock.

I trailed one hand down her side and over the curve of her waist before ending between her thighs. "You're so wet, baby." I ran my fingers along her soaked pussy. "Dripping for me."

She gripped my shoulders tightly as I teased her, running my fingers in circles over her clit.

"Wyatt, I need you." She panted. "Please."

"I have plans for you." I pushed two fingers inside. "And they all involve taking my time."

I looked down at her tits as they rose and fell rapidly with her breaths. Moved my fingers quickly in and out until her moans started coming quicker and she was riding my hand, chasing her orgasm.

I pulled my hand away, wanting her to come on my tongue like she had the night before.

"Turn around."

Her brows rose as intense desire swam in her eyes. "What?"

"Turn around. On your hands and knees. Ass in the air."

I gave one cheek a swat as she turned and got into position, then knelt on the floor and spread her wide before burying my face between her thighs.

"Oh my God." She screamed as her hips bucked against me.

I pushed hard against her clit, circling it with my tongue. She matched my rhythm, writhing with pleasure as I continued to work her over, not letting up even when spasms racked her body.

My cock throbbed painfully. I desperately wanted to feel her gripping me. Feel her wet heat pulling me in deep. I stood and fisted my cock, rubbing the tip along her slit.

Fuck, that felt amazing. I groaned before slowly inching forward. "Baby, you feel so good. And damn, this ass." I swatted one cheek, loving the moan that slipped from her. "You like that?"

"Yes," she panted as she pushed back against me. "Need more."

I slapped her ass again. "I want to savor every minute of this." Another swat as my cock disappeared another inch. "Take my time with you." I gripped her hips and pulled almost all the way out. "You'll need to be patient, baby."

"But I need you." She looked at me over her shoulder, and I all but lost it.

The desperation that matched my own was all-consuming. I could take my time after giving us both what we craved.

In one quick motion, I thrust forward until I was seated fully. We both moaned, and I pulled back and slammed forward again. "Fuck, baby. You're so tight and wet. You feel amazing." I pistoned in and out several times, eliciting sounds from her that I could spend the rest of my life listening to.

I froze, deep inside her. *The rest of my life*, I repeated in my head.

She was it for me.

The realization drove me on as I took her with so much intensity I hoped she could feel what I was feeling. I tilted forward, grabbing hold of her tits and tweaking her nipples as I drove into her again and again.

When I felt her gripping me tighter, I pulled all the way out and gave her ass another slap. "Get on top." I lay on the bed next to her. "I want to watch you as you come on my cock."

She smiled as she scooted closer and threw her leg over me. "Now it's my turn to tease you."

"Sounds perfect to me." I dug my fingers into her hips and guided her over me.

She pressed her palms into my chest, and I raised my own hands to cover hers as she lowered herself.

"You're so beautiful like this."

She rose up and sank back down, rotating her hips as she did. I groaned from the sensations she was causing, never wanting this to end.

I watched in awe, studying her features, her movements reminding me of when she rode my face with abandon. Her head was thrown back as she found the right spot, sending us both closer to the edge. She felt so good. Every time my cock dragged against her walls, I wasn't sure I would last much longer.

"Baby." I waited until she looked back down at me. "I need you to come. You feel too good."

She smiled, grabbing one of my hands and bringing it to where we were joined. "Touch me, Wyatt. Make me come."

Hell yes. And I loved that she wasn't afraid to tell me what she needed. What she wanted.

I moved my thumb in circles around her clit as she began

moving quicker up and down my shaft. She threw her head back again, and I squeezed her hand still under mine.

"I want to watch you." My voice cracked as I held on to the last thread of control I had left, ready to explode inside of her at any moment.

She looked down, and I pushed harder against her clit as she rotated her hips.

"Right there."

I groaned as her pussy gripped me tighter, and the last thread I was holding on to snapped as my pleasure swamped me and I exploded, emptying inside her as she bucked hard against my thumb, riding out her own orgasm. We rode out the waves of ecstasy before she finally collapsed on top of me.

That was the most intense encounter I'd ever experienced, and I was ready to do it all over again.

I hugged her tightly to my chest. "Angie?"

"Yeah?"

Jesus. Those three words were on the tip of my tongue. But I had no idea how she felt or if hearing them from me would freak her out. I was a little surprised it wasn't freaking me out. But I'd never been this sure before.

I blinked. Fuck.

There was another conversation we needed to have. Although, to be honest, that didn't scare me as much as it should. Being with her forever. Marrying her. Having babies with her. None of it freaked me out. All of it felt right.

Chapter Twenty-Two

ANGIE

WYATT ROLLED us so we were both lying on our sides facing each other. He popped up on an elbow, rubbing his hand up and down my arm.

"I messed up, baby."

I swallowed. Please tell me he wasn't regretting what we'd just done. I couldn't handle that.

He pressed his lips to my forehead. "I don't regret it, so get that thought out of your head. It was the best feeling I've ever experienced. But we should probably talk about it."

"Talk about it?" We had amazing sex. He wanted more than

only sex, right? I wasn't sure what we needed to talk about. But the concern in his voice had me on edge.

"Yeah." He pulled back and looked down at me. "I forgot to grab a condom."

My body sagged with relief. Surprisingly, that hadn't crossed my mind either. "I'm on birth control."

He nodded. "I would never do anything to hurt you. I've been tested recently, and I'm good. But you're also the only person I've ever not used a condom with."

I raised up on one arm. "Really?"

"Yeah." He chuckled. "I never forget. But with you, I was so engrossed in how amazing it felt, I didn't even think about it."

He traced my nipple with one finger and a shiver raced through me.

His gaze darkened as he followed his finger over my breast and down my stomach. "God, I can't wait to do that again."

My mouth fell open as I glanced down between us, locking on to his already hard cock. "Now?"

He smirked as he rolled me to my back. "Unless you need a minute." His hand cupped my breast and he claimed my mouth, swallowing my moans as his thumb flicked back and forth.

I was already panting and moaning by the time he climbed on top of me and was pressing against my entrance. He was more deliberate this time. Lying flush on top of me and moving in and out of me slowly, sensually. My nails dug into his back and our tongues tangled.

Sex had always been just sex. Nothing special. Until now. This felt so different. I understood the term making love now. The way he touched me. Kissed me. It was so much different from how anyone had ever been with me.

"Baby," he whispered against my neck as he continued to

move, lifting up to look down at me. "You're mine now, you know that, right?"

I smirked. "Hmm. Yours?" I moaned and arched up as he hit that sensitive spot deep inside.

"Mine, Angie." He stared at me, his gaze piercing with an intensity that I felt in my soul. "Tell me. Tell me this is real. That you're my forever."

I swallowed at the meaning behind his words. I wanted that. So much it hurt. But was I able to trust it? To trust this feeling?

He brushed the hair off my forehead as he searched my face. "Need to know you feel this too. This insane connection between us. Tell me I'm not crazy."

I smiled. That I could do. "You're not crazy. I feel it too. And I want nothing more than to be yours."

I left off the forever, afraid to trust in that and have it ripped away from me. But deep inside, I hoped for it.

I gripped him , my core tightening as he began to thrust harder and faster, bringing us both back to the edge again before we tumbled over together. Blissfully.

WAKING up in his arms made me just as happy as falling asleep in them had. Not quite as happy as when he woke me up in the middle of the night, though. Slipping back into me and making love to me again. I snuggled into his side, throwing one leg over his.

"Ready for round four?"

I gasped and looked up at him. "You're joking?"

His smirk said he might be, but he shrugged. "How about I go make us coffee and breakfast while you get a shower, and then we'll see. I might be tempted to let you ride my face again."

Heat crawled up my neck and into my cheeks. "I liked that."

"I know you did." His hand trailed down my back and he squeezed my ass. "Go get your shower before I change my mind and have my way with you again."

I giggled and climbed up so I was straddling him, his hard cock nestled against me. I slid over it, already wet for him again. He sat up suddenly, tangling his hand in my hair and bringing my mouth down to his.

I jolted when his hand landed harshly on my ass.

"Shower. Before I keep you in this bed all day and let the hotel run itself."

I sighed and climbed off him before heading to the en suite. When I came out to the kitchen, he was standing at the stove, his phone tucked into the crook of his shoulder.

"Yeah, I know," he said and then glanced over at me. "I'll talk to her." He sighed. "I understand. I'm not a complete idiot, but I appreciate the heads-up."

What did he need to talk to me about now? I braced for bad news.

"Seems like the trolls are at it again," he said as he turned toward me and set the phone down on the counter. With his arms crossed and jaw locked, he studied me. "Paul has me paranoid that this could be a deal breaker for you if it keeps up. I want to say I'm willing to give you that out if it's what you want. But the truth is I would rather burn my social media to the ground than let you walk away. So please tell me this isn't going to be an issue. I wish I could prevent it, but I can't."

"Trolls?" I tilted my head. "I might need more context."

His brows furrowed. "You haven't checked your Instagram yet?"

My body shook as I laughed at his statement. "Um, no. That will never be my thing. I rarely use it and only check it when someone tells me to. I upload a picture every now and then."

"Oh." He shifted. "Well, don't."

"Another picture of us?"

He nodded. "Yes. Coming out of Starlight Pi last night. Comments are cruel. Don't read them."

"Attacking your playboy status still?"

He looked away, not willing to meet my eyes. "My dating history is in there, yes."

"What are you not saying?"

His whole body screamed uncomfortable, and now I couldn't stamp down my curiosity.

"I can go read them if you don't want to tell me." Not that I really wanted to, but I would if he couldn't tell me.

"Mean comments that have absolutely no truth to them and that I refuse to even repeat."

"About me?"

"Yes," he gritted out.

"Why?"

He shrugged. "I don't really know why."

I looked down at my hands as I fiddled with the hem of my sleep shorts. "Do they have to do with my weight? The fact that I'm bigger than the girls you usually date?"

I gasped as he closed the distance and stopped directly in front of me. His hands threaded through my hair and he cupped my face with his palms.

"Nothing they said was true. Do you hear me?" His thumbs caressed my cheeks. "I love your body. I think your curves are sexy and you are beautiful. Anything else is a lie."

A tear slipped from my eye and he brushed it away with his thumb.

"Baby, please. Don't cry. I wish I could stop it." His arms wrapped around me and he brought me flush against his body.

"But anything I say or do could make it worse. The best thing to do is ignore it. Eventually they'll get bored and move on."

I nodded against his chest. I understood what he was saying, but it didn't make me feel good. Everyone would always look at us and wonder why he was with me when he could have any beautiful woman he wanted.

Through breakfast, I tried to put it at the back of my mind. But I didn't do a very good job, and Wyatt could sense it too. Although he wrapped me in his arms and kissed me until I was breathless, he didn't try anything more. I was a bit relieved, sure I wouldn't be able to be fully present for that.

Once we were downstairs and I got busy handling things it was easier to forget about. At least until my sister started texting rapid-fire.

Izzy: Fucking trolls. Ugly ass women. Inside and out based on my top-notch stalking skills.

Izzy: Some of them need to eat a whole pizza, maybe three, they look that unhealthy.

Izzy: Why do women do this? Why tear down other women?

Izzy: Like, do we not have enough to deal with? Unjust attacks from other women shouldn't be one of them.

Izzy: I mean, do they really believe you were planning to finish off three pizzas and whatever else was in the bags by yourself?

Izzy: The answer to that is no. They don't. They're bitches. Ugh. I'm sorry. I love you.

Izzy: Also, you're gorgeous. And the way Wyatt is looking at you. Wow. Just wow.

. . .

UNTIL THAT MOMENT I'd refused to pull up my Insta. But after that last text... I couldn't help myself.

The moment the picture filled my screen, I could see immediately what she was talking about. Desire, and something much deeper, was etched in his features as he looked at me. I refused to let anyone ruin that, so I took a screenshot, cropped it, and put it as my background. I was proud of myself for not reading the comments.

ME: Thank you.

Me: Are you all moved in?

Izzy: Yes. Although the guys are even more convinced the apartment is cursed now.

Me: What do you mean?

Izzy: When the first picture circulated of you and Wyatt earlier this week, they told Jay it proves it.

Me: They're ridiculous. Curses aren't real. And living in an apartment isn't the reason Owen, Jay, or I have found someone.

I ROLLED MY EYES. The apartment I took over from my brother Jay had been his friend Owen's before that. They'd each moved out after finding the loves of their lives and moving in with their girlfriends. I didn't believe the apartment had a love curse. Or maybe it didn't scare me like it did all the single guys my brother worked with who hadn't wanted to take over the lease and jeopardize their bachelor status. Now, however, I was starting to wonder. But just a little.

ME: I'm guessing they think you're next?

Izzy: Yup.

Izzy: Logan was kind of a jerk about it. Said something about me being too young. Like too young for what?

Izzy: He's so broody every time I'm around. Apparently he's not like that at the firehouse or with the guys.

Izzy: Pretty sure he finds me annoying.

I smiled as my fingers flew across the screen.

Me: Or he finds you hot and he knows Jay will kill him so he tries to be a jerk when you're around.

Izzy: He doesn't give any of those vibes. Like not even an inkling.

Me: He might be really good at masking it.

I glanced at the time and then shot off one last text.

Me: Have a meeting in a few. I'll call you later.

By the time I'd finished my meeting with a potential client looking to book their family reunion, helped at the front desk, and then dealt with a housekeeping issue, it was already late afternoon. I'd seen Wyatt in passing a few times, but only when other people were around. I was worried people might treat me differently when I came down this morning, but so far no one has said anything or acted weird.

I pushed through the door that led out to the pool area and the beach access. It was March and the pool was still closed for the season, so it was pretty much deserted. I needed a moment to catch my breath, and the sand between my toes sounded good.

I kicked off my heels and carried them with me down the path that led to the water. Standing barefoot in the sand, letting the wind whip around me, I sensed someone behind me and I smiled, hoping it was Wyatt. I relaxed into his chest when his strong arms wrapped around me.

"Next Saturday I have a Gala to attend in Boston." He buried his nose in my hair, his lips close to my ear. The warmth of his breath against my skin sent a shiver down my spine. "I want you there with me."

I spun in his arms, looking up at him. "I don't have a dress with me."

"Not a problem. I'll give you my credit card and you can go get one."

"I should have one at home. And I need to go get my car and my stuff anyway." It would be the perfect reason and opportunity for me to finish my move from my old apartment to my new one.

A sound almost like a growl vibrated through his body. "I want you to go get something new. Pick out something you love. Let me do this. Let me spoil you."

I hesitated, but ultimately, I very well might need something new. I couldn't remember the last time I wore one of my formal dresses. Did they still fit?

"Okay." I nodded. "Will you go with me?" In my experience men didn't like shopping, but I wanted his opinion.

The smile he sent me had mischief written all over it. "Definitely."

I arched a brow.

"But I make no promises that I'll keep my hands to myself."

I rolled my eyes. But I'd be lying if I said I didn't love that he couldn't seem to keep his hands off me.

His fingers trailed up the back of my shirt and I shivered when the cold air hit my skin. Warmth replaced the sensation when his mouth claimed mine. It was all-consuming, but at the same time, not enough, and I couldn't wait until we were back upstairs in his bed again.

He broke the kiss, his eyes so dark I could barely make out the green in them. He turned and pulled me along the sand back toward the hotel, utter desperation in his movements.

I couldn't stop the giggle that slipped through my lips as I hoped he had the same idea when he stopped in front of the elevators.

"I'm suddenly starving," he said as he jabbed the button.

The doors opened and he pulled me inside. Once the doors closed, he backed me against the wall and claimed my mouth again.

We were both breathless when the elevator stopped. "Can't wait to taste you on my tongue."

The giddy feeling I'd experienced last night was back as we made our way down the hall to his suite. And there was no more denying that I had fallen in love with this man.

Chapter Twenty-Three

WYATT

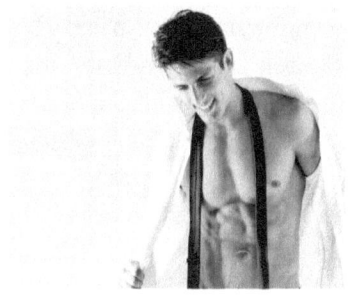

THE LAST TWO days had consisted of getting my hands on Angie any chance I got and working together running the hotel. Steven was currently taking the reins while I tagged along to help Angie pick out a dress for the gala.

So far she'd come out in two black dresses. Both accented her figure and made me shift uncomfortably on the bench outside the small dressing room.

I'd grabbed a red one off the rack. With her blond hair and always painted red lips, she would make it look sexy as hell. The look she gave me said she didn't agree. But she didn't argue about trying it on for me. It was cut low in the front so her gorgeous tits would be ready to spill from the top.

"I'm not sure about this one, Wyatt," she called loudly from inside the small changing room.

"Let me see it. I'll be the judge of that."

"You're biased and only like that it shows off my boobs."

Damn right.

The door opened wide and I let my gaze roam down her body. As I expected, the deep V gave a nice view of her large breasts, pushing them together and providing a nice valley I was imagining my cock sandwiched between.

It hugged her curves snuggly, but not overly tightly, and that was probably the part she didn't like. She didn't want to show off her hips and thighs, she wanted to hide them. I wanted her to be comfortable but also know how sexy she was.

I stood and pushed my way into the dressing room, silencing her gasp with a finger while I quietly closed the door.

"Wyatt," she whisper-yelled. "If they know you're in here they're going to think we're having sex."

I smirked. But I wasn't ready to tell her my plan quite yet. Not until I had her ready and willing to take my cock. "Face the mirror, baby."

She raised an eyebrow. "Why?"

"I want to show you how sexy you are."

"Wyatt," she whined.

"Turn around." I gripped her hips and urged her to spin toward the large mirror that hung over the bench.

"This right here." I trailed the tip of my finger down the curve of one breast into the valley between them. "This is meant for my cock. All night, that's what I'll be imagining. My hard-as-fuck cock nestled right here between your breasts."

Her eyes drifted closed as I ran my finger back up along the curve.

Using both hands, I cupped both mounds, pushing them

together another inch. "Can you picture it, baby? You in this dress, gripping me tight as I fuck your tits."

I moved my thumbs over her hard nipples, eliciting a moan from her. "Shh... You need to be quiet."

Her eyes popped open and she stared wide-eyed back at me in the mirror as I slowly lifted the dress.

"And this pussy?" I slid my hand under the silky fabric of her thong, teasing her clit. "Bare and ready for me. Because you won't wear panties under this."

"I won't?"

I shook my head. "It shows the panty line. Even the thong."

"Yeah, because it's form fitting." She laid her head back on my shoulder as I moved my fingers in a circle. She was fighting back her typical loud vocal noises I was used to hearing from her. "Too form fitting."

Using both hands, I tucked my fingers into the waistband and inched her panties down her legs. "It hugs this gorgeous ass of yours. and I like the idea of knowing you're wearing nothing underneath the whole night."

She tensed. "Wyatt," she said breathlessly, "we can't."

Funny thing was she made no actual move to stop it. She was enjoying herself just as much.

"I think we can." I raised one eyebrow at her in the mirror as I grabbed the fabric of the dress and hiked it back up around her waist, showing off her glistening pussy. Already soaked for me. Waiting for me. "All night I'll be tempted to hike this dress up and take you like this." Using one hand, I guided her to lean forward. "Hands on the bench. Let me see this ass."

She glanced over her shoulder at the door, pulling her bottom lip into her mouth. "What if we get caught?"

"Baby, trust me. Lean forward."

This time she didn't hesitate and leaned forward, her bare ass presented to me like a fucking gift on Christmas. At the moment, I was the luckiest man in the world.

I quickly unzipped my pants, pulling my cock out and running the tip through her wetness. "Can you be quiet?"

She nodded and my gaze zeroed in on her tits spilling out of the top of the dress, exactly as I'd imagined. "Look at those tits. Do you see how fucking amazing they look?"

She stared at herself in the mirror, her blond hair framing her face and red lips. Reminding me of a pin up model.

I pushed forward in one quick thrust, making her breasts bounce from the movement. "I want you to watch me take you. Watch how sexy you are. If you close your eyes or look away, I stop."

She narrowed her eyes, but I quickly pulled out and slammed back in. Her mouth dropped open, and I did it again, causing her to bite down on her lower lip this time.

"Are you watching?" I dragged my cock out slowly. "Do you see what I see?"

I hoped she was getting as much pleasure from watching us like this as I was. Damn. I needed some mirrors in my bedroom, because this was fucking amazing.

Her gaze zeroed in on us as I continued to move in and out of her warm, wet pussy. She moaned softly, and I didn't fucking care who heard us at this point. I picked up the pace and reached around to finger her clit. I was already close.

Voices sounded nearby and I paused, covering her mouth with my hand when her eyes widened. A heartbeat later, the attendant moved back to the front of the store, and I began to thrust into her like a madman.

She opened her mouth, and I pushed my finger inside, letting her bite down. Fuck. She could draw blood for all I cared. I needed her to come. Her pupils blew out as she watched in the mirror while I slammed into her again and again.

She tightened around me, spasms beginning to rock her

body, and I lost it, emptying my release deep inside her, continuing to thrust, letting us ride out the waves of pleasure.

I kept us in that position but guided her to lean back up so I could cup her breasts and she could see where we were joined.

"Do you see what I see now?" I pressed my lips to her shoulder. "I saw the way you watched us. You liked that. You liked watching me fuck your gorgeous pussy, didn't you?"

She nodded, her face still flushed red. "I liked watching."

I pulled out, tucking myself back into my boxers and zipping up my pants. "My vote is the red dress. But get the one that will make you feel sexy."

She nodded and stood facing herself in the mirror. I turned and cracked the door, making sure no one was standing there before exiting and taking my seat again.

Five minutes later, Angie appeared, fully clothed and holding the red dress.

With a smirk I raised a brow. "You sure?"

"All night I'll be thinking about it." She glanced around and lowered her voice. "What we just did. And that will make me feel sexy."

"Good girl," I said as I stood and wrapped an arm around her shoulders. "Now let's go get dinner. I must have worked up an appetite or something."

She shook her head as we made our way to the checkout counter. The woman eyed me as I stepped up to the counter, a flush rising to her cheeks. "Oh, didn't realize you two were still back there." She glanced back and forth between Angie and me with a knowing smirk but didn't say anything.

Once we stashed the dress in the car and were back on the sidewalk, Angie looked over at me. "She knows."

"Yeah, I'm sure she does." I grasped her hand and we walked down the street. "And maybe I'm wrong, but I think you liked the possibility of getting caught. Of someone seeing us."

She was quiet before a sexy chuckle slipped from her lips. "I'm finding that being with you is making me want and like things I'd never even considered before."

"Is that a good thing?" I didn't want to constantly push her past her comfort zone, but I had to admit I loved that she felt safe and comfortable enough with me to explore new things. That I was getting to be her first in so many different ways.

She squeezed my hand. "Yeah. It is."

I pulled her into my side, wrapping my arm around her shoulders, and pressed my lips to her temple.

She giggled. "I'd never done anything like that before."

"Me either."

She stopped and whirled on me, her mouth hanging open. "Like at all? I assumed—I mean…"

I gripped her chin between my thumb and forefinger, making sure I had her attention. "Nothing that comes anywhere close to what we just did. Sex has always been just sex. But with you, it's intense. It's all-consuming. I can't think about anything other than getting inside you, making you come."

Her cheeks flushed again, and I brought her lips to mine.

Pulling back, I searched her face. "With you it all feels different. I feel different."

I wasn't sure I was doing a good job of telling her how I felt, but she smiled up at me with a look that I hoped meant she was feeling the same thing.

I tucked her back into my side and we continued down the sidewalk.

"So about tomorrow."

I gritted my teeth. I didn't like the idea of her leaving. She needed to, I understood that, but I hated that she would be gone for almost three days.

"You sure you don't want me to go with you?" I opened

the door to the restaurant, ushering her in ahead of me. "It's a long drive back from North Carolina."

"No. You need to stay here to run the hotel. Besides, you said you had a dinner event Monday night for the hospital."

After indicating two people to the hostess, we followed her to a table and took our seats. "I told you I could skip that if you wanted me to."

She shook her head. "No. I'll be fine. I'll fly back tomorrow, spend the day on Monday packing, and then drive back Tuesday morning."

I wasn't going to push the issue. I already sounded like a clingy boyfriend. But, honestly, I didn't want her to go.

"I could hire movers for you."

She giggled. "You're ridiculous."

"I'm serious." I grabbed her hand across the table and entwined our fingers.

"Oh, I know you're serious, but that's also why I said you're ridiculous. You are not paying someone to pack my crap and drive my car back here. I'm perfectly capable."

I frowned, still hating the idea of her leaving but knowing she wasn't going to give in to my crazy-ass idea either. Although, I didn't think going with her was that crazy of an idea.

"Phone sex?"

She laughed loudly, garnering attention from tables around us. I smiled. It was worth a shot.

"Maybe if you're a good boy I'll consider it." Her nose wrinkled. "On second thought, it might be weird with my sister Izzy there. It's a one bedroom."

I chuckled and closed my menu. It didn't take long to order and get our food. While we ate, she told me all about her firefighter brother Jay and their younger sister Izzy.

For the first time, it struck me as funny that this was something I thought I wouldn't be good at—listening and paying attention, small talk and conversation. With Angie, I was great at it. Wanted to engage in it. I wanted to know everything about her. What she liked and what she didn't. Her family, friends, hobbies. All of it.

I blinked as she leaned forward, smirking at me. Crap. I'd zoned out. Well, obviously, I still had that issue. At least the thoughts I got lost in were still consumed by her.

Chapter Twenty-Four

WYATT

IT HADN'T EVEN BEEN two days since she left and I was already going insane. I'd just talked to her on the phone, but it didn't matter because she wasn't here. She'd be back tomorrow, I reminded myself. Then I had five days to talk her out of moving into the apartment she was going to rent. I knew it was going to take a lot of convincing, but when I thought about it, none of it made sense. We both knew she would be at the hotel with me every night. Wouldn't it be easier for her to not have to travel back and forth every day? Bottom line was I couldn't imagine her not in my arms every night.

I nodded my head at one of the other donors as he looked

expectantly at me. I hadn't a clue what he'd said, but luckily, a nod did the trick. I didn't even want to be at this damn dinner meeting. But since I was a donor, not to mention all of these people loved my grandparents and they wanted to name the new wing after them, I didn't have a choice. I tipped my head to the bar, excusing myself from the discussion. Only way I was getting through this was with plenty of alcohol. I ordered another whiskey on the rocks and cherished the burn as I tossed back half the glass.

Out of the corner of my eye, silky red fabric caught my attention, and for a brief minute I thought it might be my sexy temptress in red. I was sorely disappointed when I turned and found Natalie sidling up to the bar. The smile she directed at me made my stomach turn. At one time I thought she was totally my type, but now I couldn't understand what had attracted me to her in the first place.

"Want to get out of here?" she cooed.

She ran her hand up my arm, and I flinched back. Was she serious? I'd turned her down the last time she was standing nearly naked in front of me. What made her think anything had changed?

I studied her face as she shifted closer, alcohol heavy on her breath.

"Come on. It's always good between us." She trailed her fingers up my hand that rested on the bar.

I moved it out of her reach and placed a hand on her shoulder to stop her from falling into me.

She was drunk. Most definitely wasted. I glanced around to see if she was with anyone, and no one paid us any mind. Turning back to Natalie, I eyed her as she wobbled on her heels, her eyes red and glassy.

With a huff, she lifted a hand, attempting to flag the bartender down. I shook my head, silently telling the dude he shouldn't serve her.

"How about I give you a ride back to your apartment?"

That got her attention, and she spun on me with a smile. "As long as you come up."

I shook my head. "Not gonna happen. I'm with someone now."

"Yeah, okay." She waved me off. "You'll get bored and move on soon enough," she slurred.

I pulled up my text thread with Paul, letting him know I was ready. "Come on. Let me get you home."

She pouted and narrowed her eyes at me before sighing dramatically. "Fine. I was bored with this place anyway. Everyone is married or taken." She glanced around before cringing. "Or old."

She pushed away from the bar and stumbled forward. I reached out and grabbed her by the elbow, steadying her before heading to the door.

Once we were outside, I almost regretted trying to help her when she spun and tried to run her hands up my chest.

I locked my jaw and pried her hands off me and nodded to the waiting car. "Get in, Natalie."

She stomped her foot like a child who'd been told no. "You're no fun."

Thankfully she gave me no trouble as I helped her into the back seat. The look Paul shot me, however, said he planned on giving me an earful. I climbed into the front seat. The last thing I wanted was to give Natalie any chance to throw herself at me again.

Paul pulled away from the curb, silently stewing.

"She's drunk. Just wanted to see her home safely." I looked over at him. "You know how I feel about Angie."

He narrowed his eyes. "Right. Even more reason to keep your distance from other women. You could have called her an Uber."

"In Starlight Bay? You can't be serious."

He shrugged. "Or you could have left her there. She's not your problem anymore."

"Not my style, and you know that. I couldn't live with myself if I could have done something and didn't and then she ended up on the eleven o'clock news."

"You better hope and pray that it doesn't get back to Angie that you were seen leaving tonight's event with another woman."

My spine stiffened. Fuck. I didn't even consider that. I tried to push the unease away. If someone said something, I would just explain to her what happened. She'd believe me. Wouldn't she?

Chapter Twenty-Five

ANGIE

IT FELT good to be only a few hours away from Starlight Bay. I was beyond excited to get there and see Wyatt. Talking to him on the phone earlier wasn't long enough. My cheeks felt warm as I thought about all the things he said he'd do to me when I got home.

Home. I liked the sound of that.

My phone chimed with a text where it was mounted to my dash. I clicked on the notification and read the messages from Izzy.

. . .

Izzy: What the fuck?

Izzy: I'll help you bury the body.

Izzy: Turn around and come home. Screw that place and that playboy asshole.

WHAT THE HELL was she talking about? I hit the dial button and turned on the speaker.

"PLEASE TELL me you're on your way back," she said, skipping any type of greeting.

"Izzy, what are you rambling about now?"

"The picture of Wyatt and a chick in a red dress leaving a restaurant together last night."

My stomach sank. He said he had a dinner for the donors of the new wing of the hospital. "What picture?"

She sighed. "Let me guess. You haven't checked Instagram yet today."

Why was it so hard for people to understand that I didn't live on social media? Sure, I wasn't the norm, but I couldn't believe I was the only one.

"No. Of course I haven't. And my phone is at 10 percent, so get to the point."

"Hold on, I'll screenshot it for you. But you might want to pull over. It's bad. They look very, um, comfortable with each other."

Did I even want to see it?

I shook my head. Izzy was probably making it into something more than it was, I was sure of it. I held my breath, but the minute the picture came through, it all came rushing out on a whimper.

Wyatt

"GOD DAMMIT." I threw my phone down on my desk and pushed back my chair until it slammed into the wall behind me. "She's not answering. Why isn't she answering?" I stood and headed toward the door to my office, but I stopped when Paul stepped into my path.

He was fucking right. Being a nice guy last night blew up in my face. I couldn't lose Angie. I was so fucking in love with her it killed me to think I might have messed it all up.

"Calm down." Paul gripped my shoulder. "Relax. You said she doesn't check Instagram regularly, so she probably hasn't seen it. When she gets here, you can explain what happened. I can back you up if needed."

"Then why isn't she answering?" I brushed his hand away and moved past him. "I have to talk to her."

"What are you going to do?" A scoff followed his words. "Drive south until you happen upon her?"

"Maybe." Or better yet... I spun back to him. "Is there a way we can track her phone?"

He rolled his eyes. "You need to take a breath, not go off half-cocked."

"What if she saw it and decided not to come back?"

His face softened. "I get it. You're scared of losing her. But I'm just saying you don't have any information yet. So give it a little bit of time." He glanced at his watch on his wrist. "What time did she say her eta was last time you spoke?"

I took a calming breath before speaking. "Five o'clock."

"Good. So, you have less than an hour to wait. Then we'll know better what's going on."

"I can't lose her. I can't." The thought had my stomach in

knots. And now I was kicking myself for not telling her I loved her. Because now I wasn't sure I'd get the chance.

He stepped closer and put his hand back on my shoulder. "You won't. You'll explain. Then you'll grovel. You won't give up until you make it right."

I let my shoulders relax and gave him a clipped nod.

The next forty-five minutes moved at the slowest pace ever. Maybe part of it was that any chance I had I was either checking my phone or staring at the front door of the hotel waiting for her to appear.

I was crossing the lobby on my way to my office when the bell above the door chimed. I froze.

Angie.

A heartbeat later I was moving quickly toward her before stopping only inches away, searching her face for any indication she was pissed.

"I need to tell you something," I blurted. It might be too late, but I needed her to know nothing happened between us. That she was it for me. I had no interest in any other woman.

"Does it have to do with Natalie?"

My body suddenly felt weighted down. She knew. I swallowed and nodded, hoping she'd hear me. Believe me. I would do whatever I needed to in order to fix this. "It's not what it looks like."

"Okay."

I blinked. "Okay?" Nothing in her tone said she wasn't being genuine. But... "You're not upset or worried something happened?"

She tilted her head. "Should I be? Because if you tell me nothing happened, I'll believe you."

"Nothing happened." I stepped forward and lifted my hands to cup her face. "I am so in love with you and there's no one else I will ever want. I have spent the last hour scared to death of losing you."

She wrapped her arms around my back. "I trust you, Wyatt. All I thought about after I saw that picture was that you weren't looking at her the way you look at me." She sent me a shy smile. "You love me?"

"Yes." I regretted not telling her before she left, and I wasn't going to make that mistake twice. "I should have told you days ago, but I was worried it was too soon."

"I love you too." Nervousness etched her features. "But next time tell me when things like this happen so I can be prepared. Because while I'm not on social media, my sister spends all her time on it and will see that stuff immediately."

"Noted." I leaned down and pressed my lips to hers, savoring the moment. Relieved that she trusted me. That she wasn't holding my past against me.

A throat cleared, breaking apart, and I turned to see Paul standing nearby with an eyebrow raised.

"All good?"

"Yes," I said on a relieved sigh as I bent to pick up the duffle she'd dropped at her feet. "Come on, baby. Let's get you upstairs."

She giggled as I pulled her quickly toward the elevators. Once inside, I asked her, "Why weren't you picking up your phone if you weren't mad at me?"

"Sorry. My phone died and my charger was in my bag in the back."

I wrapped my free arm around her shoulder and pulled her flush into my side, pressing my lips to her temple, finally feeling relaxed for the first time in the last two hours.

Now I needed to convince her to live here with me. I smiled as I thought about exactly how I would do that.

Chapter Twenty-Six

ANGIE

I THREW a pair of Spanx into the open suitcase that sat on the bed. Wyatt immediately picked them up and threw them behind the bed. Sometimes sharing the same space with him was exhausting, although most of the time it was perfect. Right now, though, it was exhausting. Not only was he not packed, but he kept thwarting my attempts to pack.

"Wyatt." I slammed my hands onto my hips and narrowed my eyes at him. "I cannot wear a bridesmaid gown without Spanx."

He raised an eyebrow at me. "Who says? Did Sarah demand that?"

My brother's fiancée was so far from the demanding type it wasn't even funny. But that wasn't the point.

"No. But—"

"You didn't wear them with the red gown for the gala two weeks ago."

"Only because you demanded I wear nothing underneath," I scoffed. "And then pouted when I tried to argue."

He smirked. "From what I can remember, that worked out to your benefit."

"That's not the point."

My cheeks heated as I thought about what we did in a housekeeping closet of that hotel. It was also the turning point for our relationship in the media. Multiple pictures were posted of us in a very positive light, and most of the comments agreed we were adorable and very much in love.

"I think it is." He climbed off the bed and crowded my space, slowly backing me up against the wall. "Covering this pussy"—his hand trailed under his dress shirt I was wearing and slid between my legs—"means no orgasms for you."

I let my head fall back against the wall as he teased me with his fingers. This was exactly how he'd gotten his way when he wanted me to live here with him instead of the apartment I had rented. Reminding me what living here with him would mean. And of course, he was more than willing to pay whatever it cost to get me out of the rental. Not that I put up much of an argument. I didn't want to be anywhere but here with him.

He stepped back and smirked at me, and my chest rose and fell with rapid breaths.

"I'm taking my Spanx." I narrowed my eyes at him again. He wasn't winning this one.

He shrugged. "Fine. But I guarantee I'll have you taking them off before the end of the night."

"As long as it's after pictures and the ceremony." I moved

toward him and placed my hand on his chest, pushing him back until he was seated on the bed. "Then you can do whatever you'd like to me."

"Whatever I'd like?" He gripped my hips and guided me to straddle his lap. His thick cock jumped in his sweatpants, and I rubbed myself against it.

"Mm-hmm." Now I didn't even care if we weren't packed yet. Although I should, because it was almost midnight and our flight to North Carolina was early the next morning.

"I thought you said we needed to pack?" His fingers dug into my sides, stopping me from moving. "You said I wasn't allowed to distract you until we were packed, remember?"

I pushed hard on his chest, and he fell back on the bed with a chuckle.

"I remember." I rotated my hips, pulling a groan from him. "But you didn't listen and stopped me from packing anyway. Twice now."

"I should probably let you get back to it then."

I matched his smirk with my own. "Yeah, maybe you should."

His gaze darkened as I continued to move back and forth. Suddenly, he sat back up and threaded his fingers through my short locks, pulling my mouth to his. There was no more teasing. Just intense desire and desperation.

It never mattered if we'd just been together, we were always desperate for each other. He pulled back to look at me and I ran my hand through his dark hair. The look in his eyes mirrored my own.

"I love you," I whispered.

A smile crossed his face. "Love you too, baby."

He claimed my mouth once more and rolled us so he was on top. I could tell this was going to be different from the sex we'd had a few hours ago when we'd first come upstairs for the night. That was a different type of desperation as we'd hastily shed our clothes and he bent me over the sofa, slamming into me from behind.

This was slower, more intimate, and all thoughts of packing were gone because this feeling was all-consuming.

Being with him was all-consuming.

Epilogue

ANGIE

LESS THAN SIX months ago I watched my brother Jay get married, and now he was here at my wedding. I smiled as he twirled his daughter, Nora, around the dance floor. Maybe not biologically his, but in every sense of the word his.

Now Izzy was the only one left, but I was sure her current situation would have her married within the year, too, if not sooner. Maybe the guys were right and there was some sort of love spell on the apartment. I still didn't think their plan to talk the new guy, Seth, into taking the apartment next was that great of an idea. But they were convinced getting laid would help his grumpy disposition and this was the way to do it.

"So happy for you." Izzy pulled me in for a brief hug. "You've definitely had a whirlwind romance."

I raised a brow at her. "And you haven't?"

A blush rose to her cheeks. I knew she wasn't sure about all that. They'd had quite a few bumps, and a lot to overcome, but things had progressed between them quickly and they seemed good now.

"Can I interrupt?" Wyatt said as he stepped up next to me. "I was hoping to dance with my wife."

"You two are adorable." Izzy smiled. "She's all yours."

She made her way back to her date and I turned toward my husband. Each time I thought or said that word it felt surreal. Him proposing after two months surprised me, but it didn't stop me from saying yes because I couldn't imagine a life without him.

Even more surprising was when I mentioned wanting a summer wedding and he suggested we get married this summer. Waiting a year wasn't something either of us really wanted to do.

Wyatt's arms wrapped around my back, pulling me flush against his body as he began moving us to the music. I laid my head on his chest, melting into his hold.

"I finally understand."

I pulled back, raising a brow at him. "Understand what?"

"Why brides act like bridezillas." He pressed his lips to my forehead. "They just want everything to be perfect."

I couldn't argue. Getting married on the beach and then having the reception in the hotel I've adored since the first moment I laid eyes on it was pretty damn perfect.

"You're such a romantic." I chuckled.

"Only because of you."

I laid my head back on his chest and we moved to the music, holding each other close.

Everything had been perfect, and I couldn't have asked for anything more.

Man of the Month Books

Return to Starlight Bay, the first Man of the Month Club small town. Revisit old friends and fall in love with all new book boyfriends in this romantic seaside town full of Happily Ever Afters.

My One & Goalie by Kara Kendrick
Heavy Petting by Rose Bak
Brewed Awakening by Havana Wilder
Cupid's Beau by Imani Jay
Purrfect Planning by Tamrin Banks
Boss Me Not by AJ Ranney
Played by the Fool by Natalie Arthur
A Good Egg by Annee Jones
The Umpire Strikes Back by Logan Chance
Pour Timing by Carolina Jax
Dare to Love by C. N. Marie
Strings Attached by Stella Bella
Meow and Forever by Leah Braemel
Sinfully Sweet by Matilda Martel
Fore Better or Worse by Ellen Brooks

Beehive Yourself by Alexandra Hale
Beards & Boudoir by Heather Lauren
The Parent Pick-up by Jill Brashear
Forever the Bully by Layne Daniels
Single Dad Hottie by Annie Charme
Perfect Chemis-tree by Gail Haris
Christmas in Starlight by Robecca Austin

Get all the books!

More By A J Ranney

Note from the Author

Dear Reader,

THANK YOU for reading *Boss Me Not*. This reformed playboy and curvy heroine were so much fun to write! Hope you enjoyed them too!

My next release will be Angie's sister, Izzy's story. I'm so excited for hers to kick off a new series: Half Moon Lake Heroes: Red Line Series. You won't want to miss this single dad/nanny romance!

I appreciate each and every one of you. It's only because people like you read our books that authors like me get to publish them.

Check out my website for bonus content and stay up to date with latest releases.

Love,
AJ Ranney
www.ajranney.com

Acknowledgments

Like always, I need to thank my husband first. He has been one of my biggest cheerleaders, is always willing to listen to what I write, and has done bedtime with the kids more times than I probably realize. I appreciate your eagerness to help me when I'm stuck and your willingness to let me read to you.

And then to my kids, who are always curious about what Mommy is writing. And yes, you still need to wait until you're eighteen to read them. But by then I doubt you'd want to!

Jenn, I know you're sick of my stories by the time we get to this part! Regardless, thank you for dealing with my constant *how do I fix this?* questions and talking me down every time I'm ready to burn everything I write. You're always willing to read and edit multiple times, hold my hand when I need it, and tell me to just do it when I need that too. But above everything you've done, your friendship has meant the world to me.

A HUGE thank you to my author friends who have supported me in so many ways, whether through encouragement or reading my stuff: Annie Charme, Kat Long, Jenni Bara, Brittanee Nicole, Daphne Elliot, Kristin Lee, Amanda Zook, Alexandra Hale and many more!

Also to all my beta readers: thank you for always willing to read and give feedback! You definitely helped make Hattie's story so much better with all your feedback! Couldn't have done it without you!

Michelle, a HUGE thank you goes out to you. Every comment you left that made me stop and think, even when I wanted to push back. Your guidance really helped shape and mold this book. Thank you for always willing to answer questions or help me talk something out!

Holly, as always, thank you for being my sister, even if not by blood—and to my mom and mother-in-law: You have been so supportive throughout every step of this crazy journey!

And finally, thank you to the rest of my friends and family who have helped or supported me. I used to think it took a village to raise little humans, and that still holds true, but it also takes a village to write and publish a book!

About the Author

A.J. Ranney lives in Maryland with her ever-growing zoo, including two kids, two cats, an attention-loving dog, a bunny, a cricket-eating lizard, and her lovable, well-meaning husband. She likes to leave the chaos of her real world behind and lose herself in a steamy romance novel. Her passion for reading romance prompted her writing journey, leading her to create relatable happily ever afters that come from her own dreams and experiences.

She loves coffee, sushi, wine, and her family. Not necessarily in that order. Her inner peace comes from the water, always relating to her zodiac sign, the Pisces. It's no wonder the small town she created in her stories is situated on a lake.

Follow Me

Come be apart of my Facebook Group.
AJ's Book Nook

Find me on social media:
Instagram.com/a.j.ranney
Facebook.com/ajranney19
tiktok.com/@ajranney3
Goodreads.com/AJ Ranney
http://www.ajranney.com